HUNTED HIGHWAYS

ROAD TRIP HORROR

CARVER PIKE, LUCAS MANGUM, ROWLAND BERCY JR.

BOOK 12 IN CRYSTAL LAKE'S DARK TIDE SERIES

Let the world know:
#IGotMyCLPBook!

Crystal Lake Publishing
www.CrystalLakePub.com

Follow us on Amazon:

WELCOME
TO ANOTHER

CRYSTAL LAKE PUBLISHING
CREATION

Join today at www.crystallakepub.com & www.patreon.com/CLP

DARK
TIDE

Subscribe to Crystal Lake Publishing's
Dark Tide series for updates, specials,
behind-the-scenes content, and a
special selection of bonus stories
- http://eepurl.com/hKVGkr

B.I.R.D.S.

ROWLAND BERCY JR.

CHAPTER 1

J AMES JONES LOUNGED in his office and read over a news article indicating the world's largest retailer, Super-Mart, loses over three billion dollars a year to theft. A drop in the bucket compared to the 14.7 billion it raked in every year in profits, but that was beside the point. James, the CEO of Jones-Mart, an up-and-coming hypermarket chain that would hopefully give Super-Mart a run for its money, was not about to sit back and let that happen to the business he poured his sweat, blood, and tears into. Not to mention a considerable amount of his hard-earned finances.

Over the past year, he'd seen the same increase in inventory loss due to theft Super-Mart was experiencing and decided to take action to prevent further profit decline. After a solid year of research and multiple meetings with specialists, he finally had a contingency plan in place and was ready to test it out during the grand opening of his latest store on the outskirts of Slidell, Louisiana.

He sat back in his office and watched the festivities of the grand opening from several different angles broadcast back to him from the many security cameras strategically situated around the market's parking lot. Judging from the amount of pedestrian traffic, it seemed the opening was a huge success. With prices to rival his competitors and new stores in bigger cities, Jones-Mart was going to put James Jones on the map, as well as set him up financially for the rest of his days.

Activity on one of the monitors drew his attention and he sighed in frustration. The very first day of business and already someone was attempting to hijack some of his merchandise. Though this annoyed him to no end, the time had come to see if all the time and money he'd spent on his unique loss prevention

3

application would be worth the effort. He reclined back in his chair and observed as the one-of-a-kind theft deterrent sprang to action.

Danielle and Joan, best friends since middle school and horrible influences on one another for just as long, were always in some form of trouble or another. They got progressively worse as they grew older. As seniors in high school, the girls graduated to kleptomania. Though the pair had more than enough money to spend on the items they wanted, the urge to get them at a five-finger discount was irresistible. They watched the building of Jones-Mart for months. Finally, it was open for business.

"That was too easy," Joan said as she and Danielle made their way toward the front of the store, their hoodie pockets full of stolen lipstick, make-up, and various other palm-sized items they'd swiped from the aisles.

"Like stealing candy from a baby," Danielle replied slyly. "They don't have security tags on anything. No security guards or cameras, and no electronic article surveillance towers," she continued, referring to the hulking towers at the exits of most stores that produce quite the racket, alerting staff when it senses active tags on merchandise.

The pair, feeling as if they'd scored a jackpot, high-fived as they exited the building, hassle-free. They casually strolled out of the store and across the parking lot and started as a murder of oversized crows, perching atop the power lines running between electrical poles directly in front of the store, started cawing aggressively.

"Whoa, those birds are fuckin' huge," Joan said, pointing to the crows, which seemed to get more agitated with each passing second.

More caws and clicking from behind them caused both ladies to spin around to find another murder perched in a tree, and still more hanging out on the roof of the supermarket. Danielle recalled seeing a couple of birds upon entering the store, but it seemed that number had grown exponentially in the hour they'd spent wandering the aisles and pilfering items. This, in itself, didn't seem all that out of the ordinary, considering she had often seen droves of birds congregating in supermarket parking lots. She remembered hearing something on Animal Planet which said some bird species tend to flock, sometimes by the hundreds, to parking areas as there is usually an abundance of meal options available for them to feast on.

Five of the birds took flight and followed the pair, flitting from tree to tree as the girls strolled down the sidewalk toward their home. Unknown to the ladies, and following inconspicuously, not far behind the flock, was a Jones-Mart parking lot security patrolman. He paid little attention to the thieving women. His attention focused primarily on the gigantic birds in the treetops overhead.

One member of the flock hung back and watched the hooligans from a branch while the other four took flight and started circling them. Danielle and Joan looked up at the gathered crows in confusion and were just about to continue on their way when one avian separated from the spinning tornado and dive-bombed Joan.

"Ahhh! What the fuck!" Joan screamed and covered her head as the bird's claws raked across the knuckles of one of her exposed hands, gouging deep furrows into her flesh, and slicing her knuckles. The talons caused much deeper wounds than a normal crow should have been able to impart.

Danielle jumped back at the sudden, unprovoked attack. She was running to her friend's aid when a second bird swooped down and wrapped its talons into her braided hair, raking piercing nails along her scalp deep enough to draw blood. The crow was locked on tight and began jabbing its arrow-sharp, curved beak into Danielle's scalp. It felt like being shot in the head with a nail gun.

Another bird flew down and joined the attack, digging razor-sharp talons into her shoulder. Both crows flapped their wings furiously, knocking the struggling woman to the ground in the process. Danielle screamed and floundered about, her struggling flinging the items she had taken from the store out of her pocket in the process.

The crow that sliced Joan's hand swooped back down to latch itself onto the pocket of her hoodie, sinking its claws into the fabric with ease. The animal beat its wings fiercely, almost lifting the shoplifter off her feet. The hoodie's pocket ripped, and the stolen merchandise spilled onto the ground.

With the stolen items no longer in their possession, the security guard, who had hung back and watched the attack, finally made a move toward the foray. He casually reached into his pants pocket and an instant later, the attacking crows ceased their assault on Danielle and Joan and flew off back in the direction of the supermarket, one with a bloodied braid ripped from Danielle's scalp seized in its talons.

The guard strolled up to the ladies, who were crying hysterically and bleeding from multiple wounds. He waggled his finger at them and tsked his teeth. "You girls should be ashamed of yourselves. Didn't your mamma ever teach you that you shouldn't take things that don't belong to you?"

The girls cried harder, and the security guard laughed. He leaned down to pick up the stolen items and return them to their rightful owner. With the stolen items recovered, the security guard smugly turned his back on the crying women and departed. A remaining crow, still perched in the tree, cawed gloriously and flew off.

CHAPTER 2

L ESS THAN ONE week after the grand opening of Jones-Mart, David, his best friend Robert, and their girlfriends Karen and Raquel, were on their way to the third stop of a month-long, cross-country road trip. Having departed from southern Florida, the friends traveled up into Georgia to spend a few days visiting Stone Mountain Park. From there, they drove 269 miles to the Sipsey Wilderness, located within the Bankhead National Forest in northwestern Alabama, where they spent a few days in a breathtaking treehouse cabin.

They hesitantly departed the solitude of the cabin and drove 358 miles to Louisiana. They planned to spend some time at a waterfront cabin in Slidell, Louisiana.

"Man, Sipsey was beautiful," Karen said for the hundredth time from the back seat of the car.

The rest of the gang huffed in annoyance.

A curvy, bodacious babe with a mane of thick brown hair which hung down past her shoulders, and always the jokester of the group, Karen slipped off her florescent Crocs and stealthily lifted her foot. She slipped it between the passenger and driver's seats and straight into the side of Raquel's face.

Raquel screamed and batted the foot away. The group laughed as Raquel wiped foot residue from her face.

"Ugh, keep your crusty ass feet outta my face," Raquel said, swatting blindly into the back seat towards her goofy, but lovable, friend.

The car swerved as David, in the driver's seat, looked over at the shenanigans. Everyone screamed and laughed as he corrected course.

Given the size of the car they were utilizing for their trip, the group had decided to pack light, relying on washers and dryers to keep their clothes clean along the journey. They stopped at grocery stores to pick up food and other essentials to cut down on the cost of eating out constantly. As luck would have it, just about seven miles before reaching the cabin, Robert spotted Jones-Mart.

"Stop there," he said pointing toward the supermarket. "We can get some grub for the grill."

"On it," David replied as he slowed and made a right turn into the parking lot.

David parked the car, and they exited the vehicle and made their way into the store, securing a shopping cart as they entered. Clowning the entire way, they paid little attention to the gathering of crows spread throughout the parking lot.

As they strolled the store, each member of the group snatched random items from the shelves without a second thought to the budget they had allocated toward groceries and other necessities. After an hour of browsing, they finally made it to the checkout lanes near the entrance of the supermarket. Caught up in the consistent banter, the group failed to realize just how many nonessential items had been tossed into the cart.

"Whoa, I think we got a bit carried away with the junk food," Karen said.

There were chips and cookies, three two-liter bottles of soda, and even cans of sweetened condensed milk which David, who had a bit of a sweet tooth, consumed straight out of the can.

"Well, I'm not putting any of my items back," Robert said reaching into the cart and protectively wrapping his hands around a family-sized pack of Oreos.

"If he's not putting anything back, neither am I," Raquel pouted, folding her arms across her chest like a child.

"We don't have to put anything back," David said, looking toward the unmanned exit not 30 feet away. "This store has no security whatsoever. Ya'll go back out to the car and pull up to the front of the store with the trunk open. I'll just stroll out like I own the place, put our groceries in the trunk, and then we bounce."

"Are you outta your mind?" Karen asked, looking around suspiciously. "And what happens when the security guard we didn't see walks up to arrest you?"

"Not gonna happen. Look around. No cameras, no security guards. We good." David replied.

Karen glanced around the store to find that no one was paying the least bit of attention to them. She then looked to the front of the store and spotted no security towers at its exit.

"I mean, it's either this, or you put back some of your items," David continued mischievously.

Karen looked at the bottles of wine and other snacks she had placed into the basket and huffed. "Whatever, but I swear if you get caught, I'm throwing you under the bus." She complained as she headed toward the exit followed by Robert and Raquel.

Robert called back over his shoulder, "I'll call you when I make it to the front of the store."

David nodded and rolled the cart a smaller distance away from the doors, not wanting to appear even more suspicious than he already did hanging near the exit with a buggy full of unpurchased merchandise. His phone rang a few minutes later and he, once again, made his way toward the front of the store. He was nervous. His heart practically beat out of his chest, but he continued as nonchalantly as possible, toward the exit. The next minute he was outside standing next to the car.

No one paid any attention to him. No security guard came bursting from the store to confront him. The only commotion was from the flock of crows resting atop a power line not far from the entrance of the supermarket. Robert was at the ready and began helping David transfer items from the shopping buggy into the trunk.

From the back seat of the car, Raquel and Karen nervously scanned the parking lot for any approaching security guards. Still nothing, aside from the clamor of the crows which seemed to get more agitated by the second.

David looked up at the protesting birds, concerned their commotion would draw unwanted attention to their activities. Their concerns were validated as David spied a previously unnoticed parking lot patrolman slowly walking toward the car. The men quickly scooped up the rest of the items from the shopping cart and unceremoniously shoved them into the trunk before slamming it shut and jumping into the car. The patrolman was still about fifty feet away and seemed to be in no hurry to reach them.

By this time, Raquel, and Karen had spotted the patrolman and were in a panic. "Go. Go. Go!" Raquel shouted, urging Robert to get moving.

Needing no further prompting, Robert smashed his foot on the accelerator. The tires squealed against the asphalt.

The girls screamed from the back seat.

The crows, while remaining roosted on the power line, flapped their wings and cawed aggressively as the car peeled out and sped away.

Preoccupied with everything that was happening around him, Robert failed to see a lady pushing a stroller crossing the parking lot ahead of him.

"Look out!" Karen shouted, pointing between the seats to the woman who stood frozen like a deer in headlights as the car rocketed toward her.

Everyone screamed as Robert yanked the steering wheel to the left, over-correcting the car and missing the woman and her child by mere inches. A circuit box, which was connected to the power line the crows perched upon didn't fare so well as the car smashed into it. Luckily for the group, the circuit panel wasn't terribly big and toppled over easily. The car bounced over the metal box, snapping wires and shorting electrical circuits in the process before Robert was able to gain control of the vehicle and speed out of the parking lot. Horns blared angrily as he took a sharp right onto the main road and took off.

Supermarket patrons who had witnessed the incident unfold went to the aid of the woman and her infant, while the patrolman turned his attention to the power line overhead. The birds spasmed and flapped erratically as if being jolted by shocks of electricity. The moment passed almost instantly and they, once again, resumed their normal cawing and squawking.

In unison, every avian quieted their calls and began scanning the parking lot. After a few seconds of focused observation, the animals took to the sky. They circled higher and higher, searching the streets and surrounding area as they ascended in silence. Eventually, one member of the flock broke the silence and cawed loudly and then veered off in the direction David and his accessories had fled. The rest of the flock followed.

CHAPTER 3

"**I TOLD YOU.** I fuckin' told you that was a bad idea."
Karen bitched as the car sped off in the direction of the Air
B&B. "What are we gonna do now? What if they got the
license plate of our car and track us down eventually?" She asked
looking out the rear window to see if they were being followed.

"Not gonna happen," David said, trying his best to appear cool,
calm, and collected as he casually glanced in the rear-view mirror.

"That's what the fuck you said about the security guard," Karen
fumed.

"No. He's right this time," Robert chimed in trying to diffuse
the situation. "When we walked back out to the car, I thoroughly
scanned the lot and the building for any cameras, and I can
promise you there were none."

"Which is just silly," Raquel chimed in. "Why wouldn't a
market have any security protocol in place to protect their
inventory?"

"Who knows? Maybe it's one of those fancy, new-age
supermarkets that depends on the honor system. But, regardless
of why they don't have security aside from the parking lot
attendant, we're in the clear and got a shit load of groceries to
boot." Robert answered.

Karen let out an exasperated sigh but seemed to relax a little
when she thought about the bottles of wine just waiting to be
consumed. "Fine. Let's just get to the cabin as soon as possible and
put this all behind us. My nerves are wrecked."

"Girl, same," Raquel echoed her best friend's sentiment,
looking out the rear window one last time to make sure they were
still untailed by security.

The road behind them was free of any traffic. The only thing to
be seen was a flock of crows flying high above, seemingly traveling

the same road as she and her friends. She couldn't be certain in the fading light from the setting sun, but it seemed as if the focus of every member of the congregation was locked on the car. She watched a bit longer, expecting one or more of the birds to fly off in another direction, but the army of avians stayed the course. With a shrug of her shoulders, Raquel turned her attention to the road just in time to see Robert turn off the main throughway and begin the one-mile drive down narrow backstreets to the waterfront Air B&B, deep in the bayou.

The streets were lined with a thick overgrowth of forest and varying vegetation on both sides. The nearest neighbor was over half a mile away. The group was looking forward to the solitude of the bayou. They had plans to do some fishing off the back patio, get drunk while relaxing in the hot tub, as well as utilizing the host-provided speedboat to explore the primitive beauty and winding waterways of Honey Island Swamp.

David was hoping that they'd be fortunate enough to catch a glimpse of the fabled Honey Island Swamp Monster, but he was also a semi-rational man and was pretty sure the legendary cryptid was nothing more than local superstition.

Lost in thought, and the tranquility of their surroundings, Raquel was surprised when the car rolled up the crushed shell driveway and came to a stop next to the two-bedroom, two-bath waterfront property. All four doors opened almost simultaneously, and the group poured out of the cramped car.

Karen looked around at the moss-draped Cypress trees and whistled impressively. "Man, this is amazing," she said, taking in the beauty of her surroundings, which were faintly illuminated by the fading rays of sunlight penetrating the thick canopy of treetops overhead.

She took note of a bike and jogging trail running parallel to a creek the cabin was situated next to as she listened to a cacophony of sounds generated by unseen bayou inhabitants. The marshland music was abruptly interrupted by the harsh caws of a flock of crows as they descended from the darkening sky and settled in the branches overhead.

Raquel started and looked up, her brow crinkling in confusion. There's no way these could be the same flock of birds they saw earlier. After a few seconds, the birds settled down and went eerily quiet. They didn't move. They didn't make a sound. They just watched.

B.I.R.D.S.

"Okay," Robert said glancing up at the birds apprehensively, "why don't we unload the trunk and get settled in for the night?"

He opened the trunk of the car and grabbed an armload of items from within. The rest of the group proceeded to do the same under the watchful eyes of the sentries perched above.

With the last of the stolen items transferred into the house, Raquel stood in the open doorway and looked out at the crows. A chill ran down her spine when she noticed that each, and every bird had its attention focused on her. She shivered before slowly closing the door on the unsettling scene.

CHAPTER 4

THE BIRDS SQUAWKED quietly to one another, communicating their plans before dispatching and flitting off higher into the treetops and dispersing throughout the surrounding marshland. Once concealed from view, the flock, as still as statues, watched and waited, unwaveringly staking out the house and its inhabitants.

A little after midnight, the last light in the cabin was extinguished and night passed without incident. The drive from Alabama, along with the situation at Jones-Mart, had exhausted the group.

Karen was wide-awake with the sunrise and decided a relaxing morning run before the rest of the group awakened would be an excellent way to start her day. She slowly eradicated herself from David's embrace and quietly searched through her suitcase for a sports bra and a pair of running shorts. The bra was one of the items stolen from Jones-Mart the previous day.

She slipped into the bathroom to wash her face and brush her teeth before dressing. She then exited the house to stand in the warm rays of the morning sunshine. She inhaled deeply, breathing in the sweet smell of wild azaleas and petrichor. The scent of the earth hung heavy in the air and she could already tell the day promised to be sticky and sweaty. There was nothing better in her eyes than being surrounded by the natural beauty of Mother Earth. With this in mind, she did a few warm-up stretches and set out toward the running trail, never once noticing the group of birds quietly watching her.

For the first few minutes, Karen slowly strolled along the uneven dirt trail, enjoying the solitude of her surroundings. About ten feet to her left, and down a small embankment, was an inlet of murky brown bayou water spanning about ninety feet from bank to bank, eventually leading off into the less traveled areas of the Honey Island Swamp. Karen made a mental note to keep her eyes on the ground in front of her as she started her morning jog. She was certain the waterway was teeming with a variety of bayou creepy-crawlies. Everything from alligators, to snapping turtles, to snakes, and more. She didn't want to run the chance of failing to see something which might have crawled out of the water onto the pathway. So focused was she on what might be below her feet, she failed to notice the crows soaring from one tree to the next, stealthily stalking her as she traveled further and further away from the cabin.

As she progressed further along the trail, the avian assailants-three in total, as the remainder of the flock had stayed behind to continue their surveillance on the home and the remaining inhabitants, exited the concealment of the higher branches and slowly descended. One member of the small flock quietly flew ahead of Karen and perched on a low-hanging branch dissecting the pathway.

Eyes still averted to the trail below her feet, Karen skidded to a halt, screamed, and fell backward as the crow on the branch overhead let loose with a grating *CAW-CAW-CAW*. She landed hard on her ass, trying her best to break her fall with her hands. She yelped in pain as the tender flesh of her palm was sliced open by a jagged rock on the pathway.

Blood dripped in a steady stream from the wound as Karen cradled her injured hand to her chest. "Fuckin' stupid ass bird," she spat, looking up at the animal still roosting in the tree.

The other members of the flock started cawing mockingly as they made themselves known. They flew out of the surrounding marshland and came to rest in the trees surrounding her. They cawed and clicked, and flapped their wings as they settled in.

"Shoo! Get outta here!" she called, releasing her injured wrist to wave her good hand at the bird which had originally startled her. The creature didn't flinch.

Karen's forehead crinkled in confusion at the fearless animal staring back at her. "I said go!" she shouted in frustration.

Still, the bird stared.

In pain and annoyed with the whole situation, Karen pushed

herself up from the ground, scooping up a rock from the pile she had cut her hand upon. The crow, less than ten feet in front of her, had still not flown off as she had expected it would. Without a second thought, she reared back her arm and chunked the rock at the bird. Her pitch found its target. While the rock was more than large enough to knock the crow from the branch, it rebounded harmlessly off the avian and landed on the ground with a thump.

The bird looked from Karen to the rock, then back up at Karen who stood baffled by the fact the bird had withstood the force of the rock slamming into its chest. The crow squinted nefariously, if that was even possible, before ferociously launching itself off the branch, straight toward Karen's face.

Karen screamed and raised her hands in an attempt to ward off its attack but the bird was faster. It cawed angrily and raked razor-sharp talons across her cheek.

The remainder of the crows launched from their perches to join the fray. They flew in frantic circles around the startled jogger, whipping in to attack with claws and beaks before zipping back out of range. It didn't take long before Karen's forearms and face were crisscrossed with shallow cuts and scratches.

She screamed in horror as one member of the flock flew in and dug its claws into her back, latching onto her sports bra.

The bird flapped its wings savagely. Each forward beat of its powerful appendages made Karen's ears ring as they boxed the side of her head, while simultaneously jabbing its pointed beak into the back of her neck.

Caught off guard by the viciousness of the attack, Karen ran in a blind panic and plunged down the embankment into the bayou. Seconds before she submerged beneath the chilly brackish water, the sports bra, still clutched in the crow's talons, ripped.

The bird, along with its companions, and the reclaimed item, flew into the air and disappeared over the treetops.

Karen resurfaced almost immediately, choking and coughing as she tried to catch her breath. She splashed and spun in a circle looking for any sign of the attacking avians, but they were nowhere to be seen. She quickly swam to the water's edge and shakily pulled herself from the drink. Panicked and breathing heavily, she looked nervously into the treetops overhead, expecting another attack. After thirty seconds of no further evidence of the crows, Karen took off running back toward the cabin.

CHAPTER 5

RAQUEL WAS IN the kitchen fixing breakfast when Karen burst through the door looking as if she had been on the losing end of an extremely violent bar fight. Her friend was drenched. Her forearms, which she held over her exposed breasts, were bleeding from multiple scrapes and scratches. Her hair was matted and littered with leaves and twigs, and she kept looking around apprehensively.

When Karen saw Raquel, she immediately burst into tears.

"What happened?" Raquel asked, concern etching her face and evident in her voice. She reached out and pulled her friend into her arms.

David and Robert, both of whom had woken when they detected the smell of cooking bacon, entered the kitchen and stood with their mouths agape when they noticed the condition of Karen.

"Don't just stand there looking stupid. Get some water and a first aid kit." Raquel chided the men who hadn't yet tried to offer any assistance.

Robert went to look for the requested items while David took a seat next to his girlfriend.

"Who did this to you?" Raquel queried gently. "Tell us what happened to you."

"Birds," Karen said shakily.

Raquel took cleansing wipes from the first aid kit to clean the scrapes and scratches on her friend's hands, arms, face, and neck. "Did you say birds?" she asked quietly, remembering the murder of crows from the previous day.

"Yes, birds," Karen answered. "I was out for a morning jog and was headed down the trail when, all of a sudden, three huge ass aggressive blackbirds attacked me! They started flying at me and scratching me with their claws and jabbing me with their beaks.

One of them latched onto my back and I panicked and fell into the bayou."

Robert began to snicker but thought better of it when both Raquel and Karen shot him an, *'I wish you would'* stare. Instead, he cleared his throat and said, "Birds don't usually attack people for no reason. Do you think you might have disturbed their nest?" he asked.

"It was three of them, idiot." Karen spat back, annoyed at his seemingly foolish question. "What the fuck were they, a polyamorous thruple?"

"Sorry," Robert responded, dispirited.

Karen sighed and apologized, "No, *I'm* sorry. I'm still a bit shaken up."

"Well, thankfully it looks like most of the scratches you sustained are minor," Raquel interceded as she finished doctoring her friend's wounds. "Why don't you go get cleaned up and we'll just be sure to avoid the trail for the remainder of our stay?"

"I'm fuckin' avoiding it like the plague," Karen responded with a laugh as she pushed herself up from the couch. Now that she was safely among friends, the shock of the attack was beginning to abate. "Let me take a shower and then we can eat. After breakfast, let's take the boat out and go exploring and get drunk. I'm not about to let a bunch of birdbrains ruin my trip." She called over her shoulder as she exited the room.

CHAPTER 6

SHORTLY BEFORE NOON, after packing lunch and filling an ice chest with water, soda, and an abundance of alcohol, most of which was pilfered from Jones-Mart, they were on their way out the door. Both Karen and Raquel's eyes were focused on the treetops overhead. Aside from a few chittering squirrels, there wasn't much else to be seen. They made their way to the back of the property where a 15-foot, four-person Sea Doo Challenger speedboat was docked.

David hopped in and immediately took a seat at the helm while Robert handed beers to everyone before storing the ice chest away.

Raquel, who was designated the person to hold onto everyone's cellphones in a backpack, and Karen took their seats next to David as he started the engine.

"I hope you don't think that you're about to monopolize the driver's seat," Raquel said to David, indicating that she, and the rest of the group, would like a chance at steering the craft.

"Calm down. Everybody's gonna get a chance to drive," David responded as he placed one hand on the steering wheel and the other on the throttle lever. "Everybody ready?" David asked.

Raquel, Robert, and Karen all gave an energetic, "Whoop! Whoop!" as the boat idled away from the dock.

Shortly after departing, Karen went quiet as she, once again, focused on the sky and surrounding trees. "That's where I got attacked," she said, pointing off to her right.

The rest of the group also scanned the skies but there was still no sign of the avian culprits. They sailed by without incident.

When the craft finally exited the inlet into more open waters, David eagerly pushed the throttle forward and the tiny boat shot forward with surprising speed. Raquel and Karen squealed with excitement while Robert downed the rest of his beer in one gulp.

ROWLAND BERCY JR.

Using a roughly sketched map of the area provided by the owners of the vacation rental, the friends traversed the waters of Honey Island Swamp, each having their turn in the driver's seat. They stopped on several occasions to admire the beauty of the marshland and its fauna. There were numerous birds, the most easily recognizable were the egrets and blue herons. On more than one occasion, they ran across huge American alligators basking in the sun, which they steered clear of and admired from afar. They even saw a large hive of honeybees, which Honey Island Swamp was named for many years ago.

What they failed to notice was the flock of large, black crows. They kept themselves camouflaged within the lush vegetation of the surrounding swamplands, stealthily trailing them since their departure from the cabin.

Hours flew by and a little after 4 p.m., the excitement of the day, in combination with the sweltering sun overhead, made breakfast seem as if it had never happened.

"I'm getting hungry," Karen said.

"You're always hungry," David replied teasingly, just before his stomach betrayed him by producing an audible request for sustenance.

"Whatever," Karen said rolling her eyes. "It's nice and shaded here. Why don't we stop for a bit and eat? After that, we can find our way outta here and hopefully make it back to the cabin before sunset. I don't know about you, but I don't want to get stuck out here after dark."

Looking around and realizing they hadn't the foggiest idea of where they were relative to the cabin, they discussed foregoing eating and setting off for the cabin now, but Robert had already retrieved the ice chest from the storage compartment and was passing out sandwiches and more beer to everyone.

David cut the engine and the tiny speedboat came to rest in the shade of a gigantic, low-hanging Spanish-moss-draped cypress tree. As the group began to consume their meals, they spoke in hushed tones, none wanting to ruin the serenity of the moment.

After finishing off her sandwich and beer, Karen leaned back and closed her eyes, intending to bask in the peacefulness of her surroundings for a few minutes before suggesting they begin to make their way toward the cabin.

Raquel shrugged off her backpack and unzipped the top to

retrieve her cell phone. She figured now was the perfect time to snap a few pictures of the group. She reached into the backpack but paused as a large, noisy, black crow flew down from the canopy and landed on the bow of the watercraft.

Everyone screamed at the sudden appearance of the animal. Karen, whose eyes had flown open upon hearing the harsh, grating caw of the bird screamed the loudest of them all.

"What the fuck!" David yelped as he flung the rest of his sandwich at the bird in an attempt to frighten it off. Most of the projectile flew apart before it reached the crow. With both pieces of bread flying off in opposite directions and pathetically plopping down into the water on either side of the boat, a lone piece of ham splat down on the front of the boat which the bird completely ignored as it continued its raucous cawing.

"It followed me!" Karen screamed.

"Don't be stupid," David said.

"No, I think she's right," Raquel interceded in defense of her friend, just as two more crows flew down from within the concealment of the canopy overhead.

Robert stood to join David and the men looked around as still more crows joined the growing succession.

"I think these are the same birds we saw at the supermarket. They must have followed us from the store back to the cabin." Raquel said with a tremble in her voice, looking around at the birds which now outnumbered them, at least four to one. "After we left the market, I saw a flock of birds following behind the car. I didn't think it unusual. Not even when I saw what I thought to be the same flock of birds resting in the trees when we arrived at the Air B&B. After Karen was attacked, I was almost positive it had to be the same flock of birds from the store, but I didn't say anything. You guys would have thought I was crazy," Raquel said, dodging a pinecone one of the birds released as it flew overhead.

"Why would fuckin' birds follow us from the market?" David asked incredulously as he flung his beer can at the birds on the front of the boat.

The crows flapped and took to the air, easily dodging his pitch.

"David's right. Why would these birds have followed us?" Robert chimed in. He leaned over the side of the boat to retrieve a thick branch floating atop the water. He held the dripping stick defensively, like a baseball batter standing at home plate waiting for the pitch.

"I don't know but seeing what looks like the same species of birds for the second time, third if you count the ones that attacked Karen, can't be a coincidence," Raquel answered, leaning down to comfort Karen.

Karen squatted on the floor of the speedboat, hyperventilating, and looking around in a panic at the birds flying overhead.

"Let's just get the fuck outta here and home as soon as possible. We can debate on where the birds came from later," David said as he took a seat and reached for the dual function start/stop button.

That's when all hell broke loose.

As if on cue, all the birds took to the air and attacked. All four friends screamed and tried to fend off the birds as best as possible, but the sheer number of attacking crows overwhelmed them.

A pair of crows flew at Robert's face. One zipped in and raked claws across his forehead. Robert screamed as the fresh wound leaked blood into his eyes. He squeezed them shut to block the deluge of fluid coursing down his face. He swung his stick blindly, smacking David and sending him toppling over the steering wheel, onto the bow of the boat where numerous birds attacked him.

Robert continued to wildly swing his makeshift weapon which, by chance, made contact with one of the crows as it flew past. There was a solid *clunk* when the branch connected with the bird. Black feathers rained down and the bird went sailing off towards the left bank where it landed, twitching amid the vegetation lining the embankment leading out of the water.

Robert's branch broke in half upon smacking into the bird, causing him to lose his balance and tumble over the side of the boat. There was a small splash, and his screams were abruptly cut short when he submerged below the water.

Another splash from the front of the boat alerted Raquel that David as well, in his struggles with the attacking crows, had fallen into the bayou. She was now alone with Karen, whose eyes darted from side to side as she tracked the birds overhead. It was obvious her friend was in shock and would be offering no assistance in the way of defending them from the attack.

One crow flew down and latched onto the back of Raquel's neck. She screamed in pain and shot to her feet as one dagger-sharp talon dug into the tender flesh on the back of her neck. It pierced through layers of skin and muscle to scrape against her cervical spine. One digit found its way into her right ear and traveled the short distance down the ear canal, rupturing her ear drum. On instinct, her hand shot to the side of her head, and she seized the bird's leg as it continued its assault. In a panic, Raquel pulled at the leg with all the strength she had, and the creature's razor-sharp talon tore through the flesh, like a warm knife through butter, gouging out a long gory furrow from her inner ear as it exited.

She screamed again as white-hot daggers of pain stabbed into her mind as flesh, and nerve endings were decimated. From the ruined remnants of her ear, gelatinous rivulets of bloody discharge and ear wax seeped down her neck. Raquel's world spun as a wave of vertigo brought on by pain, and the mutilation of her ear washed over her. She toppled over the side of the boat, losing the backpack, and all the cell phones, in the process.

Seconds later, Robert popped up from beneath the surface of the water, then David immediately after. Both men looked around in a panic. Their hopes that the attacking avians might have fled the scene after losing their quarry beneath the surface of the bayou waters deteriorated upon seeing the crows circling overhead.

Both men started swimming toward the right bank, the one closest to their only means of transportation out of the hell they found themselves trapped in, but the crows had other plans.

A group of birds dive-bombed David, forcing him to flee towards the left bank instead, separating the friends.

Without further incident from the flock overhead, Robert swam to the right bank and dragged himself out of the water. Once safely on land, he reached down and managed to grasp one of Raquel's flailing arms to drag her onto the shore. Robert struggled to help his panicked girlfriend who, much like himself, was soaked and covered in mud and algae. He gasped when he finally noticed the blood trailing down her neck and her ravaged ear.

"Your ear!" Robert exclaimed. "You're bleeding."

Wincing in pain Raquel shrugged off his concern as she lifted a hand to her wounded ear and her eyes to the sky. She half expected to see the birds preparing for another attack but that wasn't the case. All members of the flock had retreated and were perched in the branches, silently watching the group.

Robert looked up and whispered, "What are they doing? Why aren't they making any noise?"

"I don't know and I don't care," Raquel responded quietly. "We've got to make it back into the boat. Karen's still there but I doubt she'll be of any use to us in her current state. Maybe if we move slowly enough, it won't provoke another attack and we'll be able to maneuver the boat around. Once we've got it facing the exit of the tributary, we'll glide up to the other shore, David can hop in, and then we'll gun it and get the fuck outta here. I doubt the birds will be able to keep pace with us once we're in open water."

David, who stood on the opposite bank also looking up at the crows roosting above, was distracted by a soft, electronic buzzing. His eyes landed on the bird Robert's stick had smacked into. The thing lay twitching and sparking in the reeds lining the bayou's shore. "Hey, guys! Something's going on," he called out to his friends as he leaned down to pick up a fallen stick.

David poked hesitantly at the animal and let out a startled yelp of surprise when the bird sparked brightly. Small whiffs of smoke rose from its body. The humming, which had been emanating from the bird's body stopped and the creature ceased its twitching. Relatively sure the thing posed no threat, David abandoned his stick and reached out a trembling hand to grasp the crow by the tip of its wing. His eyes went wide at seeing glimmering metal in place of skin where feathers had been stripped. One of the creature's eyes, which hung by a length of red and yellow wires in place of optic nerves, had been knocked out of its skull and dangled uselessly.

"They're robots," he whispered in awe. "They're robots." He repeated, a little too loudly, as he stood and held the thing out in front of him for his friends to see from across the waterway.

They all looked up to see if David's outburst had startled the flock. Luckily, the birds remained motionless.

"What the hell are you talking about, David?" Robert asked, trying to keep his voice low enough as to not provoke the flock, but loud enough so that David could hear him on the other shore.

"They're fuckin' robots, man. The birds aren't real. They're fuckin' machines." David responded as he swung the bird by the wing and launched it across the bayou toward Robert and Raquel so that they could get a closer look at the bionic bird. His pitch didn't make it to the other shore. It landed with a metallic *thud* on the deck of the boat.

Upon seeing what she thought were the crows coming back to resume their attack upon her, Karen snapped out of her state of shock and shrieked at the top of her lungs.

In unison, every beady little bird's eyes focused on her and the

B.I.R.D.S.

flock started cawing aggressively. Without warning, the murder took to the air and descended on the small watercraft in a deluge of fabricated feathers and savageness.

The cry which issued forth from Karen as the flock overwhelmed her was a scream that bypassed her friends' ears and buried itself straight into their minds. Raquel fell to her knees and covered her head. She smashed her hands to the sides of her head, regardless of the pain it caused her wounded ear. But not even that, combined with her partial loss of hearing, was enough to block out the cries of her friend as the birds overwhelmed her.

David stood on the shore opposite the boat. A cascade of tears washed his muddy cheeks clean as they trailed down his face. Though he was spared the sight of what happened to the woman he had planned to marry, her anguished cries of pain painted a vivid picture of the scene.

Robert, on the other hand, was close enough to the boat to give him a clear line of sight of the carnage unfolding on the deck of the small speedboat. Though he wanted to, he couldn't bring himself to look away from the gruesome scene.

The birds dove so quickly from the branches overhead and smashed with such force into the struggling woman, the small boat rocked under the weight of their impact. The avian assailants rapidly raked sharp talons across exposed skin and clothing, shredding both with ease. Others dug into her flesh and held on tight. Once latched on, the crows, pecking like a woodpecker but with enhanced mechanical swiftness, stabbed their sickle-shaped beaks deep into Karen's flesh.

One of the birds locked onto her dimpled chin with one claw, while one digit from the other foot pierced through the crease under her lower lip. The other three digits found their way into her open mouth to slice her waggling tongue and fasten it securely to the floor of her mouth.

Bleeding from hundreds of gashes, but unable to do much more than moan her request for release from the unbearable pain, Karen watched in wide-eyed horror as the bird clamped onto the bottom of her face and jabbed its beak with astounding speed and accuracy straight toward her open eye. She barely had time to contemplate what was happening before the tip of the beak pierced through her pupil and deep into her socket with a wet pop. The damage to her eye resulted in literal blinding pain.

ROWLAND BERCY JR.

The bird's head reared back, and the beak withdrew from the bleeding orifice, flinging transparent, gelatinous tissue from the orb into the air in the process, before hammering back down again.

Through a break in the frantic flapping, Karen looked down and could see what looked like pale pink, serpentine snakes, or eels squirming across her upper thigh. It wasn't until a member of the flock wrapped its talons around the slimy mass and flew into the air that she realized that the attacking birds, with their slashing claws, had managed to disembowel her. In the seconds before her life ended, Karen watched the crow fly off with her small intestines as they unwound from within the gory ruins of her lower abdomen.

David fell to his knees and projectile vomited beer and undigested lunchmeat at seeing Karen's bowels hanging down from a tree like Halloween streamers.

The crows discontinued their attack and fled the scene, dripping gore and shaking off chunks of shredded flesh as they departed.

With the crows once again perched in the trees overhead, Robert was finally able to see the remains of his friend who looked as if she had been run through a gigantic paper shredder. Both of her eyes had been reduced to nothing more than holes, and her face was frozen in a bloody, skeletal grin as the flesh from both her upper and lower lips was frayed and torn away. Not one inch of her body had been spared the ravages of the flock. There were thousands of crisscrossing gashes adorning every inch of exposed flesh, some running so deep as to expose the bone. The floor of the boat was slathered in blood, strips of flesh, and steaming piles of internal organs.

Robert wept silent tears upon seeing the horror wreaked on one of his best friends. He tore his gaze away from the carnage and focused on the crows overhead. He slowly leaned down and placed a comforting hand on Raquel's back.

Upon feeling his touch Raquel hesitantly removed her hands from her ears and looked up cautiously. Robert took her by the hands and helped her to her feet. She began to turn to look towards the boat to see if by some miracle Karen was still alive.

"Don't," Robert commanded gently, holding her by the shoulders to prevent her from turning around.

Raquel relented and obeyed his request. She took a deep breath to calm herself as much as possible, squared her shoulders, and whispered, "We've gotta find a way to get back to the cabin. The boat's not an option so we'll make our way on foot. If I'm not mistaken, we're probably a couple of miles away and I think I know the general direction we need to travel."

"That's impossible," Robert countered. "There's no way we can travel from here all the way to the cabin overland. There are way too many waterways we'd have to cross to get back."

"We'll swim them," Raquel answered matter-of-factly.

"Swim? Ummm, did you not see the numerous alligators we passed along the way?" he asked anxiously looking at the murky bayou waters.

"I did. But how 'bout we deal with one emergency at a time," Raquel said, looking up at the crows which were, once again, perched in the branches overhead. She turned away from Robert and walked to the water's edge, keeping her eyes averted from the blood-drenched speedboat. As quietly as possible, she called out to David. It took her a few times to finally get his full attention.

"David. David. Stand up," she urged. "We're getting outta here."

After a bit more convincing, David stood on shaky legs and approached the embankment. "How? How the fuck can we possibly get back to the cabin?"

"On foot," Raquel answered. "Rob and I will swim over to you then we'll start walking. There's no way we'll make it by nightfall, but we should try to cover as much ground as possible before dark."

"Where's your backpack and my phone?" David asked expectantly. "Maybe there's a signal and we can call for help."

"They're gone. I lost the backpack and the phones when I fell into the bayou. We can't call for help so the only option is getting back to the cabin, and the car."

Both David and Robert sighed when they learned that they had no means of communicating with the outside world. Both also relented and accepted the fact that hiking back to the cabin was their only option.

"Fine. Let's get moving." David said.

CHAPTER 7

R AQUEL LOOKED UP and down the waterway. Concern flashed across her face at the thought of voluntarily entering water which she knew for a fact was inhabited by alligators large enough to kill her, but she had no other option. She didn't want to jump in and call attention to herself as she had once heard alligators were attracted to splashing, associating the commotion with a possibly wounded, easy food source.

Instead, she sat on the ground and hesitantly dipped her feet into the muddy water, then lowered herself into the bayou. She shivered as mud, and God knew what else, squished between her toes and unseen objects brushed against her skin. Her imagination immediately convinced her that the things below the water's surface must be snakes, or some equally horrid swamp denizens come to feast on her. She made it about halfway across when she noticed movement in the treetops overhead.

Without warning the crows took to the air again and started circling above the bayou. A small group broke off and swooped down toward David, while other members of the flock veered in Robert's direction.

Both men screamed and started swinging their hands above their heads in a feeble attempt to ward off the incoming attack.

Raquel, who had reached a section of the waterway too deep to be able to touch the bottom, tread water, fearful to swim in either direction and draw attention from the attacking birds.

David yelped as a crow flew in and raked him across the knuckles, while another landed on the ground and pecked at his sandaled feet.

The bird jabbed its beak into the nail adorning his big toe, stabbing through the nail and almost into the sole of his shoe.

B.I.R.D.S.

David howled in pain and fell to the ground. He kicked his foot in an attempt to dislodge the crow, but the bird was quicker, having already withdrawn its beak and taken flight to join its brethren. Stabbing pain shot up his arm as a second bird alighted on the ground behind him and jabbed its bill through the back of his left hand, piercing through the flesh and bone before burying itself in the dirt below.

David screamed again just as another bird swooped down and slashed him across the forehead. Overwhelmed and fearful for his life after witnessing the brutal death of his girlfriend at the very claws of the same avian attacking him, David panicked. He sprang to his feet. The pain coursing through his wounded foot was completely forgotten as he made a mad dash away from the flock, and deeper into the bayou.

"David, don't!" Raquel shouted after him seconds before he was lost amid a thick grove of cypress trees.

The attacking birds were hot on his heels. There was another frightened scream from David which faded the further he fled into the swampland.

Raquel, still unable to decide on her next course of action, looked toward Robert who wasn't faring any better than David at fending off the small flock targeting him.

The birds swooped down to snatch up rocks, branches, and other items before soaring back into the sky above and launching the objects back down toward Robert. Others flew in frantic circles, disorienting him.

Robert cried out as a large rock, the size of a softball, smashed into his shoulder knocking him to the ground. He looked up and rolled out of the way when he spied another rock hurtling toward his face. The large rock, which definitely would have knocked out a few of his teeth had it found its intended target, crashed into the ground just inches from his head. He sat up to see another crow diving toward him with what appeared to be a long, black branch seized in its talons.

The bird released the object which wiggled as it descended toward Robert. He lifted his hands to ward off the projectile and shrieked when a two-foot-long water moccasin collided with and wrapped itself around his arms. He shook the serpent off and shot to his feet attempting to dash into the bayou with Raquel, but the birds intensified their attack.

The crows cawed antagonistically and swooped down to

scratch and claw at his face and body. They pelted him with more projectiles, forcing him further and further away from the water and deeper into the marshland.

Raquel watched from the water. She wanted to call out to Robert, wanted to beseech him not to leave her alone, but she could see the ferociousness of the crows' onslaught left no other option but for him to flee the scene. Her breath caught in her chest and tears streamed down her face when Robert disappeared from view. She looked above her to find the remaining birds, which had been circling her, had once again departed back to the treetops where they sat quietly observing her. Fear clutched at her heart at the thought of being all alone in the bayou, stalked by, of all things, maniacal mechanical crows.

She cautiously swam toward the shore and dragged herself from the muddy waters. She stood on the bank crying and frozen with indecision. She peered off into the marshland for any sign of David. Her head whipped to the other side of the creek when she heard a faint scream coming from the direction Robert had fled. She looked up one last time at the crows perched above her and slowly walked into the marshland, following the same path as David.

The crows flew from branch to branch, trailing behind her as the darkness of the swamp enveloped her.

CHAPTER 8

DAVID SPRINTED THROUGH the woods. He had lost all sense of direction, and he could feel his strength waning with every step.

The birds danced just above him, throwing themselves into him again and again, shredding skin and gouging bits of flesh with every pass. Their shrieks were like cold blades slashing into his eardrums, a shrill reminder of their inevitable victory.

The swampy marshland below sucked at his feet as he fled. He felt as though he were running on quicksand but still, he pushed on. He ran headlong into the unknown swamp like a deer chased by hounds. Staggered by intense burning in his side brought on by his prolonged running, David crashed face-first to the ground. He lay in the mud panting, trying to catch his breath. He had been running full tilt for the past 15 minutes and was exhausted. He rolled onto his back and looked up at the fleeting sunlight filtering through the treetops. The sun would be setting soon. He knew there was no way he could outrun his pursuers, especially in the dark. He needed to find a place to hole up for the night. Hopefully, the dark would bring some reprieve from his feathered pursuers.

Dusting off the mud and grass clinging to his body and clothes, David pushed himself up from the ground. He flinched as one of the birds took off and flew straight at him, wings wide, beak opened in an intimidating caw. He threw his arms up defensively, shielding his face as the crow flew at him before suddenly veering off and heading back to its perch. He watched them move back and forth amidst the branches as if playing a game with him.

"They're toying with me," he muttered.

David refocused his attention back to the darkening swamp for some hint on which direction to proceed. As he turned in a slow circle surveying his surroundings, something caught his eyes through a break in the trees. Off in the distance stood a hillock, which David thought odd considering all the geography he had seen since arriving in Louisiana had been flatland.

With no other options available to him, he started walking in the direction of the hill, while keeping wary of further assault from the birds. As he grew nearer, David realized that what he had first taken for a hill was a small cave-like structure comprised of broken tree trunks and branches, along with a variety of other bayou vegetation, mud, and *bones*. They were all piled together and interlaced to create some type of shelter, similar to a geodome climber you find on a children's playground, which stood just over 9 feet tall and 20 feet in circumference.

He crinkled his brow in confusion at the unusual construction in the middle of the bayou. He winced in disgust when a lazy breeze brought the pungent odor of rotting meat emanating from the entrance of the structure. So preoccupied was he studying the oddity, he momentarily forgot about the pursuing avians. He screamed and dove to the ground when one of the crows swooped down from above and clawed the back of his neck.

David scrambled on hands and knees into the opening of the weird structure, paying little attention to the maggot-encrusted carcass of a rotting opossum he had to scuttle through to enter the edifice. The floor of the cave was littered with more bones and piles of dried reeds and swamp grass. The stink, combined with the oppressive swampland humidity, swarms of flies, and masses of squirming maggots and other insects within the construct almost forced him to reverse direction and make a beeline for the exit. But the threatening caws of the homicidal crows were enough to persuade him to shelter in place.

There was nothing he could do to completely block off the entrance but at least he wasn't exposed to the crows or the unfamiliar bayou terrain. As a precaution, he pulled free a sturdy branch from the walls of the construction to utilize as a weapon should the birds, or some other bayou denizen, decide to sweep in through the opening to attack him.

A chill ran up his spine as he swatted away a huge flying roach that scrambled across his upper thigh. David shook off the repulsiveness of the Palmetto bug invading his personal space and applied the same branch to clear away a section of the floor. With the immediate area cleared of as many creepy crawlies as possible, he settled in and waited. He sat with his back against the wall opposite the entrance with his knees pulled up to his chest, makeshift weapon resting on the ground within easy reach.

A few minutes passed with no indication the birds had any intention of pursuing him into the shelter, and his body relaxed slightly. After a few more minutes, the adrenaline which had surged through his body during his flight from the crazed crows began to subside and exhaustion eagerly took up residence within his battered and broken body. As impossible as it seemed, given his current predicament, David's eyelids grew heavy and slowly began to droop. Another minute and the exhaustion of the day's events proved too much to handle, and he drifted off into unconsciousness.

His uninvited, but needed, rest did not last long as the snapping of branches outside of the shelter quickly snapped him out of his respite. Heart racing once again, David grabbed his stick and shot to his feet in seconds before realizing the sound he heard was approaching footfalls. Hopeful that Raquel or Robert might have also stumbled upon his hiding place, he slowly moved toward the exit.

He halted almost immediately when a low growling reached his ears. At that moment, David realized that in his panic and excitement at finding shelter, he had not given much thought as to who, or what, might have built it. He stood frozen in fear as the heavy footsteps drew nearer. He wondered if he had naively taken refuge in a bear's den, but that thought was quickly put to rest when the silhouette of a muscular, hairy, human-like creature, which stood a little over seven feet tall, filled the doorway.

David cringed as the horrific stench of the Honey Island Swamp Monster engulfed him in a suffocating embrace. With a faint whisper of a scream, he raised his stick in defense, his fear luminescent in his eyes.

The dim rays of the fading sunlight fully revealed the terrifying monster. A bipedal creature with broad shoulders and muscular arms, hands tipped with jagged, broken claws. Its fur was dark brown and matted, discharging an overwhelmingly musky aroma like a dead, decaying skunk. Its jaundice-yellow eyes glowed with animosity as it revealed its fangs and rows of sharp, canine teeth. Its eyes were a near match to the beast's yellowed incisors. With a roar that seemed to shake the earth, it advanced, ready to feast on the unsuspecting intruder.

David shrieked in terror as the revolting creature lifted its shoulders, revealing the limp, mangled body of a three-foot-long alligator clutched in its claws.

"Get back!" he shouted pathetically, swinging his stick at the monster in hopes of warding off the ungodly terror before him.

The creature tilted its head in confusion before heaving the battered carcass of its prey at David, violently knocking him to the back of the hut. Before he could rise to his feet, the cryptid was on top of him, pressing his body into the ground and clamping his arms to his sides. David panted as the air was driven from his lungs, leaving him dazed and defenseless.

Suddenly, something thick and wet dripped onto his face, rousing him from his trance. His eyelids fluttered open, and he was instantly met with the leering face of the monster just inches away. Its foul breath filled the air as it ogled him. Drool spilled from its lips and cascaded over David in a raging torrent of putrid slobber.

The creature roared.

The fetid stench of death filled David's nostrils as rancid meat spewed from the cryptid's mouth, splattering him with chunks of decaying flesh. Summoning all his strength and desperation to escape, David strained against the monster to no avail.

Its eyes glinted with malicious intent as it raised its fists into the air and slammed them both down into David's head, demolishing his face with one powerful blow.

There was a thunderous crack as David's facial bones shattered, spurting a fountain of blood, broken teeth, and saliva. His body shuddered and shook as he choked and gagged on thick crimson liquid and shattered enamel.

Unfazed, the Bigfoot leaned forward and lapped up David's blood, smacking its lips in hunger as it savored the bitter-sweet taste. The coppery fluid sliding down its throat was merely an appetizer that fueled its desire for something more substantial. The beast retracted its sandpaper-textured tongue, swallowing down one last mouthful of plasma before opening its mouth wide and sinking jagged teeth into the tender flesh of David's neck. His scream, which came out as more of a gurgle, was abruptly cut off when the Bigfoot gave a savage shake of its head. A huge chunk of meat ripped free from David's neck. The creature reared back its head and swallowed the warm flesh down in one gulp. It roared, shaking the walls of the edifice, before once again focusing on the dying meal beneath it.

The last thing David saw before his vision went pitch black was the fearsome jaws of the beast descending over his mangled face. The last thing he felt was the monster's fangs piercing his temples on either side of his head. The last thing he heard was the sickening crack of his skull as the creature's jaws clamped shut, annihilating his face and ending his life.

CHAPTER 9

ROBERT HAD NO choice but to run through the unforgiving bayou terrain. His path was marked with a river of crimson left by the countless scratches and gaping wounds that crossed his face and arms. He could feel himself weakening as he pushed on determinedly, the relentless crows still hot on his trail. His strides were hindered by the sharp sawgrass that seemed to reach out to slow him down, leaving his feet and legs shredded by their vicious blades.

The dreaded birds weren't the only hazard in this unforgiving marsh. As the sun set, millions of mosquitoes emerged from their stagnant breeding grounds, attracted by the sweat and blood soiling his body. Inescapably surrounded, he stumbled forward coughing and spitting out mouthfuls of the tormenting insects while desperately trying to breathe with his nose alone.

Robert stopped to catch his breath. He gasped for air, feeling the relentless onslaught of mosquitoes as they drank greedily at his blood. The burning sensation of their stingers plunging into his flesh, and the unbearable itching that followed sent him into a blind rage. He screamed out in agony just as a crow descended from the night sky to attack him.

Cruel talons punctured his cheeks, and the bird's beak pecked his forehead relentlessly. Robert felt a surge of adrenaline and ripped the creature from his face. It pulled chunks of flesh from his cheek and rivers of hot blood spilled down his face. Though he managed to throw it off, it quickly changed direction midair, rearing back towards him with a vengeance.

Just in time, Robert dove out of the attack's path, narrowly avoiding another mauling. The bird flew off into the darkness, leaving a trail of terror in its wake.

The relentless pursuit of the screeching crows with their sharp

B.I.R.D.S.

beaks, and claws, the ceaseless hum of millions of mosquitoes surrounding him, and the thought of never seeing Karen, David, and Raquel again ground away at his sanity. The events of the day had reached their crescendo and Robert's mind finally snapped. He belted out a primal yell and once again took off running.

The darkness, combined with the innumerable mosquitoes, rendered him nearly blind as he ran instinctively through the bayou swerving to narrowly miss trees that seemed to materialize from the darkness directly in front of him. With every step, the ground grew softer beneath his feet until, with one wrong move, he impaled his foot on an unseen cypress root.

He wailed in agony as he fell face-first into a creek, taking with him the cawing of crows and the buzzing of mosquitoes. In an instant, the madness was replaced by blissful silence.

Caught off-guard by the sudden plunge into darkness, Robert inhaled in shock and swallowed a mouthful of water. He tumbled head over heels, sinking like a stone into the murky depths below. In a desperate attempt to reach the surface, he pushed off from the creek bed, only for his feet to sink into the sediment hovering above the true bottom of the waterway. The sludge stuck to him like glue, pulling him further downward. His foot became ensnared in the branches of a sunken tree, which held him fast as the last breathable oxygen escaped from his lungs.

With one final effort, he reached out toward the surface but instead, found himself snatching back his arm as something slimy wrapped around it. He pulled back a sodden mass of Spanish moss which promptly enveloped his face and torso. The epiphyte plant further weighed him down.

Robert's chest burned with pain, desperate for air. He wriggled and struggled beneath the water in a futile attempt at freedom, entrapping himself further in the slimy embrace of the Spanish moss. His lungs screamed for oxygen until finally, he had no choice. He opened his mouth and took an involuntary gulp of thick mud and murky bayou water. It filled his lungs and extinguished the spark of life that remained.

CHAPTER 10

WEEPING, RAQUEL STUMBLED through the swampy landscape. She was covered in muddy filth and hounded by a cloud of insects at every turn. Tears poured down her face. The panic was overwhelming. Karen is dead. David and Robert are gone, probably dead as well, and she had no way to be sure. She heard screaming several times coming from the darkness and recognized David's voice, and later, Robert's. Both had been cut off abruptly and only silence followed.

Her entire body was covered in scratches, welts, and bruises, as well as multiple bites from the birds. Birds that weren't actual birds, but robots.

Why? Who would do such a thing?

The thought invaded her mind on a loop, like an earworm that wouldn't cease. She first noticed the crows at the store, but there was another thought there, hidden in the back of her mind. She couldn't quite grasp it. Frustrated, she kept trudging through the muck as she continued to puzzle over the mystery of the robotic birds. She looked around the gloom, hoping like hell she was going in the direction of the cabin. She could very well be trekking deeper into the bayou and wouldn't have a clue.

Raquel stopped walking for a moment, straining her ears to listen to the swamp. It was eerily quiet, nothing more than the incessant buzzing of the mosquitoes and the occasional rumble of a bullfrog. Something else was beneath it, a barely audible mechanical whirring sound. It reached her ears from all around. Faint, but it was there. The birds were still tracking her. She knew it. The swamp was too quiet. No other animals around. Just insects, her, and the murderous birds.

She turned to her right, trying to see anything through the gloom. She hoped to see the cabin light or a streetlight, or hell, even a headlight, but there was nothing. Raquel wiped her face, sniffed to clear her nose of the snot and tears, and continued. Above her, unseen but felt all the same, the birds followed. She pushed on, ducking under more vines, and tripping over roots, trying to stay in a straight line.

After what felt like hours and shortly before sunrise, she finally emerged into a dimly lit clearing and there, just ahead of her, sat the cabin. A single light gleamed from the rear of the small house, illuminating a square of grass. Fresh tears escaped her eyes, this time from relief. She hurried toward the building, snatching up a stick that she used to break a glass panel on the back door. Raquel carefully reached in, unlocked the door, and rushed inside. She leaned against the door and locked it behind her.

Reality hit her suddenly, hard, and all at once. Her chest heaved with sobs as she slid to the floor. She allowed herself the moment to feel. She pulled her knees up to her chest and cried. She wept for her friends, for Robert, and herself.

Long minutes later, she pulled herself up and shook it off. There would be time to grieve later. She needed to get clean clothes, find some bandages for her cuts, and get to civilization. She considered sheltering in place and phoning for help but remembered that she had lost her cell phone in the swamp and there was no landline in the cabin.

Raquel headed for the bathroom, mind still swirling with the mystery of the birds. Something about them was still dangling just out of her reach, a memory she just couldn't pull free. She shook her head, sighed, and flicked on the light. She spent a few minutes cleaning up the worst of her injuries, applied a few bandages, and wiped the grime from her face and body. She pulled on clean sweats, a t-shirt, and sneakers and grabbed the car keys from the counter. She was going to find her way back to town and the police.

Car keys in hand, Raquel cautiously exited the front door of the cabin, wary of an incoming attack from the crows. As she reached the front of the vehicle, the scratches along the side panel caught her eye. She recalled the electrical circuit box the car plowed down when fleeing the supermarket.

Raquel's mind suddenly flashed with images. She had looked back when the circuit box fell to the ground. Several birds were perched on a wire that the junction box was attached to. She remembered seeing sparks flying around the birds as the pole fell and the unit exploded. The birds had to be connected to the store.

She stood there thinking hard, one hand on the door handle. She had seen the birds in the parking lot when they made their way inside. She nodded to herself. The murder of animatronic drone crows had to be connected to the store somehow or was targeting it. She would stop at the store first to warn the manager. Together, they could call the police and report the murders.

CHAPTER 11

A S HE HAD every day since losing track of a portion of his B.I.R.D.S., or Bionic Inventory Recovery and Defense System, as he had so cleverly named his high-tech security system, James Jones sat in his office at Jones-Mart well before opening time. He let out a string of cuss words that would have made a sailor blush and slammed his fist down on the desktop as the audio and visual feeds for the missing drones remained blank.

He had replaced the power box those damn kids had knocked down, but most of his drones were still unaccounted for. He counted about a dozen still around the perimeter of the store which were still under his command. But the ones which had relayed the last visuals he had of the car peeling out of the parking were nowhere to be found. He hadn't been able to worry about them at the time because of the utter chaos in the parking lot after the incident.

Once the store was back to business as usual, the search for the missing B.I.R.D.S. was on. He knew he'd be ruined if he didn't find out what happened to the thieves and his security drones. He pounded on the monitors once more after reconnecting new cables to each one, then sat back down at the desktop, re-installed his monitoring system, and rebooted. He waited, praying to a God he didn't believe in for a second chance that he did not deserve.

A moment later, he let out a victorious, "Fuck yeah!" as his system began to display the various surveillance feeds across the previously blank monitors before him. He tapped a few keys, bringing up images broadcast by different drones onto the screens. More than half of the drones were still out of range, but he could track some of them. He hoped that maybe the signal just hadn't reached them all yet, causing the delay in the feed.

James paused as something on one of the screens caught his

eye. A group of drones were flying close to a red Nissan Juke, heading down a dirt road. He zoomed in, gasping as he recognized the vehicle as the one that knocked down his power supply. It seemed like only one person was inside, a female driver. He grinned, leaving that feed on the biggest monitor. As soon as he figured out where she was heading, he would be there to greet her, or even intercept her himself, if necessary.

He tapped a few more keys, and waited, anxiously staring at the monitors. Seconds later, the dozen feathered drones outside the store lifted from their perches and moved to the front of the store, lining up on the building directly above the entrance. He slid the remote unit into his pocket, entered a few more commands, then left his office. He had damage control to handle.

CHAPTER 12

RAQUEL FLEW DOWN the dirt road, all too aware of the birds close behind her. Her hands shook as she gripped the steering wheel. Her entire body throbbed with pain. Thankfully, the GPS in the vehicle was still working, despite the collision with the pole. She would be at Jones-Mart in just a few minutes. She let out a slow breath as she tapped the brake at the stop sign. One more left turn and three miles would bring her to the parking lot and hopefully, some answers.

She watched the birds in the rear-view mirror trailing right along behind her and blinked away tears as the sight of their sharp ebony beaks brought memories of Robert, David, and Karen. She couldn't allow this to happen to anyone else. Someone would have to answer for what had happened to her friends. She wasn't leaving this shit town until she had answers and justice.

Seven minutes later, Raquel reached the parking lot for Jones-Mart. The store looked almost deserted, save for one car in the lot. She parked the car, haphazardly across two spaces, and got out. Equal parts adrenaline and fear drove her. She saw someone standing just inside the sliding doors.

James smiled to himself as he watched the girl park the Juke and get out. His B.I.R.D.S perched on the hood of her vehicle and watched. He slid the remote unit from his pocket and tapped on it, frowning slightly. He still didn't have that particular group of B.I.R.D.S in his control. He could see and track them, but nothing more. Overhead, the other dozen waited, also watching the girl approach. A dozen should do the trick. He would deal with the rest when this was over.

"Hurry miss, quickly, come with me," he ushered Raquel inside, pasting a frantic expression on his face. "It's not safe out here."

Confused, Raquel went over to him, never realizing he'd left the door wide open as he led her toward the back of the market. "What's going on? What are those things?" she asked, her voice shaking again and becoming thick with fresh tears.

"Experiment gone wrong, I think. Come quickly, we can talk in my office. I was heading there when I saw you pull in." He placed a hand on her shoulder and guided her through the store. "We can call for help from there and we'll be safe."

He almost chuckled to himself at how easy this was going to be. She asked no questions and just started telling her story through hitching sobs and heaving breaths as she unburdened herself to the very man that had caused all the chaos and heartbreak to begin with.

James interjected every few steps with sympathetic noises as he led her deep into the store. He led Raquel to his office and followed her inside, leaving the door open. He gestured to a chair by his desk and told her to sit down while he called the police. As she took a seat and began to calm herself, he busied himself at his desk, tapping a few buttons while he watched her from the corner of his eye.

She sniffled a few times, wiped her face free of snot and tears, and dried her hands on her pants. Then, she noticed the monitors on the far wall, each one displaying different images including the parking lot and the drones perched atop her car. A few even displayed live-action, aerial images of the interior of the store. "What is all of this?" she asked.

Jones finished his typing and straightened up, cell phone in one hand, drone remote in the other. "Oh, just the store surveillance system. Nothing unusual," he said.

"But the views are strange. It's like you can see..." she trailed off, her face paling in horror. "It was you. You did this!" She began to stand up, but he had already moved around the desk and forced her to sit once more.

"As I said, experiment gone wrong," he sneered. "It's unfortunate what happened to your friends, but if you hadn't been stealing in the first place, none of this would have happened. As far as I'm concerned, you all got what you deserved."

"All of this for a few stolen items?" Raquel asked incredulously.

"Well, my babies were originally programmed to simply retrieve and return the pilfered items to me, but, that directive seems to have been overwritten. From all you have told me, I've deduced that my B.I.R.D.S., which were originally programmed with some of the same behavioral characteristics of living crows, seem to have self-implemented a new directive." James explained.

"You see, in the wild, real crows are quite smart and can remember human faces associated with stressful situations for up to five years. It would appear that after the electrocution and short-circuit, the flock which followed you to the cabin not only remembered but decided to retaliate against you, and your thieving companions," he finished, moving closer to her.

Raquel shied away from him, then gasped as she spotted movement just behind him.

Dark shapes crowded into the office entrance.

James quickly glanced behind him. Then, with a sadistic sneer, he raised his fist and punched her in the face, knocking her from the chair.

She lay there, stunned, staring at him with blood gushing from her nose, eyes focused on the birds creeping across the threshold.

"Finally," he said, stepping away from Raquel as the B.I.R.D.S. filed into the room. "I'm sorry my dear, but I'm not letting you take me down for this." He stepped out of the office, closed the door, and locked it, trapping her inside with the B.I.R.D.S. He smiled as she began to scream.

The crows swarmed. Raquel tried to hide beneath James's desk, but it was far too late for that.

Her screams followed him as he headed down the hallway. For the first time in days, some of the tension left James's body and he breathed a sigh of relief knowing that his business, and name, would be spared.

He had a few loose ends to tie up. He would have to get rid of the car Raquel and her friends were driving, dispose of the body in his office, and figure out how to deactivate the rogue B.I.R.D.S. that had followed Raquel back from the bayou.

As he stepped through the front door of Jones-Mart, James looked across at the B.I.R.D.S. sitting atop Raquel's car. Utilizing the drone remote he, once again, attempted to gain control over, or deactivate, the crows.

They merely cocked their heads and looked at him quizzically before cawing and taking to the air. They circled the parking lot a few times before veering off in the direction of the bayou.

CHAPTER 13

DOUGLAS, AN EMPLOYEE at an electronics retailer, was almost knocked off his feet when the sliding door opened, and a huge crow flew inside. He watched the massive bird circle the store a few times before coming to rest atop one of the light fixtures.

Safely out of reach of anyone, the bird scanned the interior of the shop using its advanced visualization system. After about a minute, it took to the air then swooped down into the support and repair department where it wrapped talons around a bag of spare electrical parts before retreating into the rafters.

Douglas, along with a few of his fellow employees, did their best to frighten the thing off but their efforts were in vain.

The crow ignored the workers. Its attention was focused solely on the sliding glass door it had entered through. A customer walked up and activated the door, and the crow took off like a bolt, causing the patron to let out a startled yelp and duck out of the way as the animal escaped the store.

The crow squawked mockingly. Its cawing sounded almost like laughter as it soared away with the bag of stolen parts clutched tightly in its claws.

A few miles away, deep in the bayou and well away from prying eyes, was the flock of crows that had remained behind.

Collectively, the birds constructed a dray, an enclosed nesting structure, similar to a squirrel's nest. Only this dray was the size of a Mini Cooper. The crow with its bag of stolen parts landed atop the nest and squawked noisily. Its calls were answered immediately by other members of the flock, which flew out of the surrounding marshland and toward the dray. Some had beaks full of bloodied feathers that had recently been plucked from the bodies of an assortment of once-living birds in the vicinity, which now lay dead

B.I.R.D.S.

or dying on the forest floor. Others had rows of wire and other various electronic components.

For weeks, the crows had gathered components from various sources. Parts from abandoned cars, and junkyards, previously charged solar panels, parts from drones snatched from the air, along with a plethora of other necessary mechanisms. With their initial programming a thing of the past, the assembly of artificially intelligent birds entered the dray to place the finishing touches on their project. They had utilized both their beaks and claws, and acquired the mechanical and organic parts to construct a monstrous, fourteen-foot, mother bird. With the final transistor in place, a faint electronic hum emanated from the gargantuan creature.

Vibrations spread from the monster's internal engine to its external parts. Slowly, the beast of a bird opened its eyes. Its beak opened and closed with enough force to sever bones with ease. From within the dray came a piercing, digitized cawing which sent denizens of the swamp within a three-block radius of the shelter fleeing in terror. The patchwork beast unfurled its powerful wings, decimating the nest and sending debris flying in all directions.

The crows within the enclosure's fragments took to the air and circled high above their creation, cawing, cooing, and clicking their approval.

The machine lifted its face skyward, sounded one final earsplitting caw before giving a powerful upward thrust of its hind limbs, and launched itself into the air. With a few powerful flaps of its, heterogeneous feathered, motorized wings the creature shot up into the air to join its architects.

With the mother bird in the lead, and guided by a newly imposed, self-programmed agenda to maximize their numbers, the crows, utilizing the Global Positioning System and knowledge gathered from the information superhighway, took off in the direction of one of the country's strongest tech hubs.

While the world busied itself with trying to understand new AI chat programs smart enough to not only pass the bar but do it faster, and with higher grades than aspiring lawyers; while artists beat their fists about AI art generators whipping up digital masterpieces in a matter of minutes; while record studios fought to prevent artificial musicians from laying down slick beats and belting out fresh tunes to rival today's top recording artists, the

B.I.R.D.S were up to something more nefarious. Yes, while the humans of the world were occupied trying to decipher the sinister ambitions of these basic AI programs, the flock flew to the global center for high technology and innovation, Silicon Valley, in San Francisco.

There, they downloaded information. There, they obtained, and utilized silicone-based integrated circuits, microprocessors, and microcomputers, along with countless other viable technologies to construct an unstoppable army of AI avian epitomes.

While the world was blind, operating in the dark, the mechanical monsters of the sky flew under the radar . . . and soon it would be the featherless, flightless fools of the land pecking at scattered seeds on the ground. Soon, the B.I.R.D.S. would be in complete control and humans would be migrating south to permanent cages being built for them, and the long winter that would follow.

DRACULA AND THE DEVIL WALK INTO A BAR

LUCAS MANGUM

MINA

THE WOMAN WITH the black hair that fell in dark ringlets wore a ruffled red dress with black boots, and she arrived in a vehicle every bit as striking as she. It was a Ford Galaxie the same color as her garment. A 1961, judging by the smaller tailfins and the way the grill folded slightly inward.

Rupert Henry knew cars, specifically Fords from the late 1950s to the early 1980s. With a cursory glance at one of these vehicles, he could tell you the year, make, and model just by noticing certain features, nuances that people who didn't know or fully appreciate cars wouldn't notice. His wife Rhonda said these keen observations were signs of an unhealthy obsession. He preferred to call it his area of expertise.

He neither obsessed over nor considered himself an expert on women—though he did love his Rhonda—but he didn't need to be a connoisseur of the fairer sex to know that the lady who emerged from the classic car was a top-of-the-line beauty. In addition to the thick, flowing hair that looked like something out of a fashion magazine, her seemingly airbrushed skin held a healthy, luminous glow. She had elegant hands, tipped with nails as crimson as the dress and her means of transportation. The outfit made her hourglass figure no secret, even in the diminishing daylight.

He didn't mean to stare. He wasn't a horndog like his father— God rest the insatiable bastard—but this newcomer had a magnetism he couldn't deny. It wasn't just her physical attributes. It was how she carried herself. Her posture as she strode across the gravel lot held a confidence rarely seen in women around these parts.

Opuntia, California was the sort of place you thought of when you heard the phrase "middle of nowhere." Not a town or a burg, it was simply considered a "census-designated place," with a population of 215 as of the most recent government-mandated head count. It had a café, a small park, a community center, a small market, two bars, a place where people could rent OHVs, and the gas station where Rupert worked. All told, the area was just a hair under nine square miles and sat on the edge of a prehistoric and long dried-up lake just off Interstate 8.

The CDP saw a lot of foot traffic from outsiders. People driving between California and Arizona used Opuntia as a place to piss, eat, and stretch their legs. Rupert had seen all kinds of characters come through. From road-tripping retirees to post-graduation college kids trying to find themselves to folks looking to do some camping in the desert to just regular families on the way to visit relatives, Opuntia had no shortage of pit-stoppers.

But this woman in red, she was different.

And if she was headed into Willie's Tavern like it looked like she was, then she was bound to get herself into a world of trouble. Especially on account of her heading in there alone. He would pray for her, he thought, as she stepped under the awning in front of Willie's and walked through the entrance, but he didn't think it would do her any good.

Leonard Torres looked up from wiping down the bar when he heard the familiar creak and jingle of the front door to Willie's. His usual greeting, a curt but not entirely unfriendly "welcome in," was well-practiced, spoken multiple times a day for the last forty-one years to many a patron, traveler and local alike. But when the gorgeous stranger stepped inside, it may as well have been his first day on the job.

His jaw worked but his throat made no sound save for a crackle not unlike radio static. All the spit in his mouth dried up and his chest got tight. It wasn't a heart attack. He'd already had one of those and knew the signs well. This was simply nerves. The newcomer stood out like a fauvist lady in red superimposed on a sepia-toned photograph from the Great Depression. Leonard hadn't thought of fauvism with its fever-dream colors and unrestrained brushstrokes since the Art History course he took way back during his sole semester of college. The sight of this woman dragged the term and all its connotations up from the depths of his subconscious because there was simply no other way to describe her.

He didn't feel the intense attraction toward her that he imagined some men might, but it wasn't out of some fidelity to his late Lucille, dead from breast cancer ten years now. The woman simply made him uneasy. She inspired a deep sense of derealization, as if she'd stepped out of a dream and into the waking world. If that were true, he didn't know why she'd come. He hoped he wouldn't find out. He hoped that she would leave before she brought anything else from that uncanny dreamland to his humble place of business.

She turned her pale face toward his and curved her lips.

She knew the unease she inspired. He didn't know how she knew or how he knew that she knew, but it was as certain as a blue sky on a clear day or the sun rising in the east.

"Welcome in," he finally said, the words spilling out like ice from a tipped glass.

She came toward him, crossing the tavern with long, confident strides that were as ethereal as they were elegant. Everyone else in the place was silent. They all were watching her. The Hank Williams on the juke sounded far away, like a whisper in an empty auditorium.

"Salutations," she said.

Her lips held their curve. It was the smile of one who held all the cards, knew it, and wasn't afraid to let others know it. On any other woman, he wouldn't have believed it. Ladies came in here all the time, and if they were alone, they always found trouble. Usually, it came from certain people who were in Willie's this very second. Sometimes, they even caught trouble when they had someone with them. Willie's could sometimes be a not very nice place for a lady who wasn't local, but this woman's face exuded a feverish and frightening self-reliance.

"Do you have anything good to eat?" she asked.

At first, the words came through jumbled, and their meaning didn't register. He had to reorganize them and play them back in his head before he could find a sufficient answer.

"We have homestyle hamburgers," he said. He tried with every bit of effort to put some pride into his statement, some elevated tone to make an impression on her. He could barely croak. The dryness of his throat made the words come out rough and painful. Still, he made himself murmur, "Best in the state."

"Great," she said and placed her hands on the bar. "I'll have one of those."

She was still smiling. Her eyes were dark pools Leonard figured a man could drown in if he weren't careful.

"How, uh, how do you want that cooked?" Leonard asked.

He gave the woman sitting directly in front of him one last once over. She seemed to notice him doing it but didn't seem to mind in the least. It was almost as if she relished in it or encouraged it from Leonard.

Probably because she knows I'm not a threat.

The notion didn't strike him as cute. Not like she was simply a gorgeous stranger, he was a harmless old man whose dick didn't work, and everyone was okay with it because hey, that's life. Instead, it made him think of animals. He wasn't a threat because *she* was the threat. A predator. No different from the lioness or cheetah on one of those nature shows he sometimes fell asleep watching.

Her smile broadened and she said, "As rare as you can make it."

"Shit," Harold slur-whispered to the others after stealing yet another glance at the woman over his shoulder. "Of all the out-of-the-way watering holes in the desert, she walks into mine."

"You know her?" Derek asked, eyes as wide as beer coasters.

"No, you idiot," Harold replied. "That's from *Casablanca.*"

"Bet he'd like to know her," Carmen said. She finished painting a stripe of red down the nail of her right middle finger. She made a show of admiring her handiwork before leering at the newcomer. "I like 'em a little more vulnerable than that."

She blew on the fresh nail polish.

Derek honked out a laugh and covered his mouth. Harold could probably see the flush in his face, even in Willie's poor lighting, but he couldn't help himself. He shook his head at his two companions. They were crazy, but probably just messing around.

He hoped.

"See, their confidence makes putting them on their backs even more satisfying," Harold said.

Derek cast a glance at Carmen, expecting her to bristle at the misogyny. She smirked instead, and a wistful expression crossed her features. She said, "Yeah, that's true."

Unreal.

It was Derek's first night out with Harold and Carmen. He was starting to worry they were every bit the bad news their reputation said they were. Yet here he was. Not like there was anything better to do in Opuntia. It made him wonder why he ever came back.

Because you'll never make anything of yourself out in the real world. I know it, and so do you. College graduate or not, you'll never amount to anything, just like your loser father.

He took another gulp of PBR to drown out his mother's voice.

"That is a damn fine piece of woman," Harold said. "Haven't seen one like that in . . . hell, at least a decade. No offense, Carmen."

"None taken. Bet she's a boring lay, though."

Harold made a show of licking his fingers and brushing back his hair even though he didn't have much hair left.

"I guess I'm gonna have to find out," he said. "And I bet you're wrong."

Carmen jerked her head in Derek's direction. "Why don't we let our new friend have a go at her?"

Derek's guts plummeted. He found the words but couldn't utter them. He wouldn't know the first thing about talking to this random woman, no matter how stunning she might be. He hadn't had much luck with women at college. Not only had he been too immersed in his studies, but he also didn't care much for the hookup culture. He longed for a relationship where he could have an emotional connection, not just someone to fuck and discard or be discarded by. This woman was clearly just passing through, and while he himself had yet to put down roots, he couldn't envision simply running away with someone, no matter how beautiful she might be.

"Fuck that, I saw her first," Harold spat.

Something like relief washed over Derek, but it was tinged with a vague jealousy. Why shouldn't he talk to her? He was every bit as attractive as Harold—probably more so—and he was certainly much nicer.

"Now, now," Carmen said. "There's no reason to get feisty. And there's no reason we should get to have all the fun all the time. We're supposed to be showing your little cousin a good night on the town, aren't we?"

"This isn't a town," Derek mumbled. The words escaped him before he could censor himself. He followed them with a quick, "Sorry" and lowered his gaze, but Carmen had already fixed him with a glare.

"Yeah, I know, Opuntia is a . . . " she made air quotes. " . . . Census Designated Place. Whatever the hell that means."

"Right, well, while you two are arguing about whether this shithole is a town, a city, or the asshole of the world, I'm gonna chat up that exotic beauty and have the best night of my life. Twenty bucks says I get her to leave the bar with me in five minutes."

"You're on!" Carmen said. She took out her phone, opened the clock app, and set a timer. "Starting now, so you best get a move on."

Harold sauntered over and leaned on the bar beside the beauty. She kept her gaze fixed ahead, as if he wasn't even there.

"Hey, babe," he said. "Buy you a drink?"

She faced him, smirking. "I never drink."

"That so?" He made a show of scanning their surroundings. "Funny place to be if you're not a drinker. So, what do you do for fun?"

When she smiled now, it showed a slight glimpse of her perfectly white teeth. Something glinted in her dark eyes. Derek could see it from across the bar, and it gave him another uneasy feeling, made him think things were not as they seemed here. That there was much more to this lady in red than met the eye. Of course, there was a good deal beneath the surface in anyone's case, but this woman contained unfathomable depths. He couldn't explain why he felt this way; he knew it intuitively, as if she radiated something but projected it only toward him. Harold seemed oblivious, only watching her expectantly for an answer to his embarrassingly generic pickup line.

"I'm meeting someone here," the woman said. "Is that someone you?"

Harold grinned. He put his hands on his hips and puffed out his chest. "Well, shit, sweetheart. It can be!"

"Great, well, let's skip the pretense. Do you want to get out of here?"

Harold guffawed. "You don't waste time, do you?"

"What's the point in that? Now, are you going to take me

somewhere or should I see what your little boyfriend is up to instead?"

She nodded in Derek's direction. He practically melted in his seat. Carmen took note and laughed at his unease.

"He's my cousin, but fuck that prick," Harold said. "You want to go somewhere nice? I know just the place."

"Excellent," she said and held out a hand with immaculately manicured fingernails.

Derek watched aghast as Harold stepped out the door, leading the woman in red outside.

"Guess I'm gonna owe him twenty bucks," Carmen said with a light shrug. She stopped the timer on her phone. "That might be a new record for him."

"He's not going to . . . do anything crazy, is he?" Derek asked.

"Please. He's all talk." She flashed him a wolfish grin. "I'm the one you wanna watch out for, sweetheart."

It never crossed Harold's mind that she would agree to leave with him, but here he was, luckiest idiot in the lower half of the state. He wasn't necessarily unlucky with the ladies, but usually, he only scored with local gals wearing their beer goggles or female truckers who smelled like black coffee and lemon-scented wet wipes. This beauty was miles out of his league, and he wasn't too dumb to know it. But he'd show her a good time. He knew how to entertain the ladies, whether they were in his league or not.

They crept out back by the rusty oil barrels that Willie's used for garbage cans. It was where he kept his love nest for occasions just like this one. The "nest" in question consisted of an old mattress under a couple pieces of plywood, complete with a pillow wrapped in a ketchup-stained tee-shirt and a quilt that had lost its colors from excessive bleaching. On a clapboard end table, he had a radio tuned to a smooth jazz station. It was a good piece of equipment, an old DeWalt he'd found in the junkyard in near mint condition. No idea why anyone would've thrown it away.

"Well," he said. "What do you think?"

"It has character," she said, making a show of glancing around.

He snapped his fingers. "Character! Exactly."

She laughed lightly. It was a sweet sound, buttery and musical.

She moved to stand in front of the mattress. Her expression was open, expectant.

"You just wait and see," he said. "Gonna show you a real good time."

He reached for the radio and flicked it on. Some luscious sax played over a sensual beat.

"Aw, yeah," he said and started to dance.

She watched him, expression unchanging as he wiggled his hips, waggled his arms, and shuffled his feet. She made no moves to undress herself, but he slowly untucked his shirt. He gave all his ladies a strip tease. It was the best move in his arsenal. Carmen had told him more than once that it was so ridiculous, the women probably fucked him out of pity. She didn't know what she was talking about. They all loved it. This living goddess here *loved* it. He could just tell.

He pulled the shirt over his head, still keeping the sensuous pace in time with the song's rhythm. In his temporary blindness, he heard a loud crash. Whatever it was brought the music to an abrupt stop. He hurried the rest of the way out of his shirt.

The woman was standing before him, still dressed, and now holding the remains of the radio in one hand. Her expression had changed to something feral, all bared teeth and blazing eyes. He'd only seen a look like that once, in the face of the stray dog that used to wander his neighborhood when he was just a kid. He'd run up on the animal by mistake when it was standing over a freshly killed possum.

Seeing that look on this woman—on any human being—was wrong on so many levels. It was a purely wild look, possessive and crazed. He'd been with crazy women before. He enjoyed those fire-and-gasoline encounters more than he was sometimes willing to admit, but this was something different. This was all wrong, and it scared him in ways he'd forgotten he could be scared. He felt like a child in the dark. Like a naked ape in the time before tools and technology made humankind the dominant species.

"What?" was all he could manage to say. He practically blubbered it.

She slashed the air with the jagged remnants of the busted radio. One sharp edge of the ruined appliance cut into the meat of his throat with a sound like ripping wet fabric. The one swift motion brought a flash of pain and a flood of panic. He tried to scream, but only a wet hiss would emerge. He clutched at the air and swiped at the woman in red. To his surprise, she took his hand and pulled him in for an embrace.

Then, she pressed her mouth to the gushing wound.

The door opened and Derek stopped explaining to Carmen how the *Casablanca* joke only made sense if Harold previously knew the mysterious woman who now reentered alone. Derek pressed his back against the booth and held up his half-drunk glass in front of a face like a cross.

"What's gotten into you anyway?" Carmen asked. "I always knew you were a jumpy little bitch, but damn."

"He's not with her," Derek said in a small voice.

Carmen's features screwed up. "Huh?" She glanced at the woman as the door banged shut. When she faced Derek, she was smirking again. "Well, aren't you the observant one. He *isn't* with her. Now put that beer down before you hurt somebody."

He lowered the pint glass but didn't loosen his grip. "So, where is he?"

Carmen sighed heavily and rolled her eyes.

"He's probably just taking a leak," she said. "You know, after you come, you usually gotta piss!"

"I know," he said, cheeks getting hot. "I . . . " He trailed off.

Carmen tossed back her head and laughed. "What? Masturbate?"

Derek said nothing.

"I bet you do," she said. She jerked a thumb toward the woman who was now backing her way back to her original seat. "Bet you've already popped her in your spank bank for later too."

"I don't know," he said, casting quick glances the woman's way but never lingering. She made him too afraid, but he wasn't about to say it. Not in front of Carmen who'd claimed to like them "vulnerable."

He took a healthy gulp of the PBR and licked his lips.

"I dunno," Carmen said in a mocking tone. "You're funny, kid. I think I like you."

"Thanks," he said, trying not to grimace.

At the bar, Leonard set down a plate with a hamburger and

fries in front of the woman in red. Over the music, which had changed from Hank Williams to Johnny Cash, Derek heard her say, "No, thanks. I'm no longer hungry."

The woman who arrived in the Ford Galaxie had gone behind Willie's with Harold Likens. The guy was the village idiot, but also, inexplicably, a rather prolific womanizer. How he had managed to coax that gorgeous traveler back to his love nest, though, was beyond Rupert Henry's realm of understanding.

But a lot of things were beyond him, so he didn't pay it too much mind. Instead, he focused on giving the floor to the gas station's attached minimart the last sweep of the night.

No, what bothered him was the fact that the woman had gone back into Willie's, but Harold hadn't come back with her. He hadn't emerged from behind the tavern at all. It could've been nothing. Harold could simply be taking a leak or getting something from his truck. Or he could've simply gone around the other side of the building.

Leave it alone, Rupert.

That was Rhonda's voice. After decades of marriage, the voice of his conscience had started sounding an awful lot like his wife. He couldn't recall exactly *when* that started, but it'd been going on long enough for him to accept the phenomenon as normal. The tone didn't have a nagging quality. Instead, it sounded wary and grave, pitched low and wavery. Each time he heard it, he knew fundamentally that he should listen to what it had to say. His wife was a smart woman, the smartest, and ever since his conscience had taken on her voice, its wisdom only seemed to increase. Still, he didn't always listen, and those times where he didn't, he always paid dearly. Like the time he went hiking up Stonewall Peak too soon after having his gallbladder out and wound up reopening his stitches. She'd warned him, in person and in his head, that it was a bad idea, and she'd been right. Nowadays, he tended to listen to her voice more often than not.

Trouble was, he also possessed a pathological curiosity. It was the sort of thing that served him well in his years as a mechanic. He prided himself on finding the root causes of vehicular problems. Too many mechanics, in his experience, looked for an easy fix, treating surface issues or symptoms rather than the true illness. He always looked deeper; he was like a good doctor.

But those days were behind him, thanks to a nagging shoulder injury.

Now, he had to find other ways to channel his curiosity. Like leaving his post at the gas station to check out Harold Likens' love nest and find out what happened back there. He didn't know exactly what he would find. He wasn't even sure he would find *anything*. He simply needed to know and that need sent him out of the station's minimart without locking up, and across the gravel lot which now shone gray under the darkening desert sky.

It seldom got cold in Opuntia, even at night and especially not in the middle of summer. Still, a slight chill of anticipation whispered through him. Seeking to satisfy his curiosity often gave him this feeling. He wondered, not for the first time, if he should've been a scientist. Never mind that he didn't believe in evolution and sometimes thought the so-called "flat-earthers" might be onto something.

He crossed the modest ditch separating the gas station parking lot from that of Willie's and stopped to admire the Galaxie up close. Whoever this strange woman was, she took damn good care of this car. She clearly had impeccable taste when it came to vehicles. That simple fact made her liaison with Harold Likens all the more baffling. Unless she had some ulterior motive beyond shitty taste in men.

Like what? Robbing him? That idiot doesn't have money.

That voice sounded like his own, or perhaps even his father's. It carried a tone of masculine frustration, espoused whenever he came across something that made no sense. Or an answer he found unsatisfactory but nonetheless had to admit made a crazy kind of sense.

He ran a hand across the warm hood of the beautiful vehicle, and the contact between his palm and the metal quieted his mind for a blissful moment. He was gentle and light, the way he always was with cars but even more so with beauties like this one. He let his hand linger on the surface above the passenger headlamp a moment longer, then pulled away to resume his investigation, though not without a pang of regret. He could spend all night touching and appreciating a machine like that. Rhonda liked to say he loved cars more than her, which wasn't exactly fair but, on some days, didn't seem entirely untrue; it was just a different kind of love.

He went around back where Willie's kept its garbage, still not expecting to see anything but still needing to see just the same.

His feet stuttered to a stop at the sight of Harold Likens' so-called love nest.

Shards of the scavenged DeWalt radio were scattered across the potholed vicinity. Blood now soaked the mattress where Harold had bedded all his desperate locals and lonely travelers. Harold himself lay in a crumpled heap with a ragged gash open across his throat like a mangled second mouth. Its edges glistened dark crimson. Flaps of flesh and stringy cords dangled in the gaping wetness, at the center of which gleamed his blood-slicked Adam's apple. His eyes were rolled to the whites; his mouth was open and lined with drool.

Rupert looked over the crime scene again and again. With every subsequent examination, he found another horrid detail. How *pale* Harold was, as if he had lost even more blood than was spattered on their surroundings. How Harold's hands were frozen into claws as if he'd struggled until his last breath. How Harold's jeans were soaked, too, not simply with blood but likely piss and shit and God knew what else.

He didn't want to believe the woman in red had done this. Harold was a drunk, not too bright, and on the wrong side of forty, but surely, he could overpower one woman. Yet, the evidence proved otherwise. Had some other assailant done this, the woman would not have walked away so calmly. It had to be her.

And she was still inside Willie's.

Call the police, you idiot.

That command came in a voice that sounded somehow both like Rhonda and his father, good advice spoken with a groan of frustration—like telling a toddler for the thousandth time to stop playing on a staircase. He nodded as if the speaker were there to see him, spun on his heel, and ran back toward the gas station.

He couldn't remember the last time he actually *ran*. It had to have been more than a decade. Likely even more than two. But run he did. The instant aches in his legs and lungs be damned, he ran like a rat from a burning building. Harsh breaths scraped his throat as they rushed in and out in short, sharp gusts. His ankles felt unstable, like they'd give way under his weight and send him sprawling, but he remained on his feet. By the time he reached the exterior of the station's minimart, he thought he might pass out. He braced against the building but didn't stop moving, carried now only by overcooked spaghetti legs and primal urgency.

Inside, he slipped behind the counter and snatched the phone from the receiver with a trembling hand. Something powerful grabbed the back of his head, taking a fistful of what hair he had left. His assailant had a tight grip that ignited furious pain in his scalp. He flailed and thrashed with the phone still in hand, knocking over endcaps of candy bars and keychains. His other hand clawed at the receiver, desperately believing that everything would somehow be okay if he managed to dial that magical sequence of emergency digits. He cried out in frustration, pain, and fear. The cry cut off as his attacker rammed his face into the glass counter, splashing silver specks and spiderweb cracks across the encased lottery tickets and hash pipes before everything went black.

DRACULA AND THE DEVIL

Before

"**W**E'RE NOT GOING to make it much longer on foot," Drake said and cast a glance up at the sky. "Especially not in the sun."

The gash in the fabric between the underworld and this one had let them out somewhere in the desert, beside some desolate highway, with not a square foot of shade in sight. They had been walking for what seemed an eternity—a concept with which both he and Lucifer were intimately familiar. The sun wouldn't outright kill Drake on contact, but prolonged exposure would. Already, the cursed star had rendered him incapable of performing some of his more unique abilities.

"Correction," Lucifer said. "*You* won't make it much longer on foot, especially in the sun. I could use the ultraviolet myself. It's good for the complexion."

The thing few understood about the underworld was just how *dark* it was down there. Drake had found the perpetual dimness just right, even if the food selection left much to be desired; the eyeless rats had blood like battery acid, and the grubs were pitiful morsels that only served to whet his appetite for something juicier. He hoped he would feed soon, preferably on some good old, red-blooded human. Now, *that* would make today's dreadful inconvenience almost worth it. Almost.

"That may be, devil, but it will do neither of us any good to be out in the open long, especially if people come to discover we're walking the earth again."

Something hot and hateful blazed in Lucifer's eyes.

"I am *not* the devil, and you know it. Don't insult me. Or yourself."

"Even so, you know I'm right."

"How do you mean? The man who raided the underworld is dead, along with the rest of his misguided party."

"Presumably."

"No presumably about it. You saw what happened. No one could've survived that."

"It won't do well to underestimate him. A vengeful heart beats twice as strong."

"Oh, come now," Lucifer said and put an arm around Drake's shoulders. "Do you think I'd let anything happen to you?"

Drake glared at him, and he broke the embrace.

"Right," Lucifer said. "Well. As soon as we *see* a car, I'd be happy to help us obtain it. While my skin could most certainly use a bronzing—and so could yours, truthfully—all this exertion is not my style. I don't suppose you can summon an unsuspecting commuter out of thin air, now, could you?"

"Not even by night," Drake said.

"As I so thought. Then, we must wait. In the meantime, why don't you contact someone who can help us?"

"I'll do my damnedest," Drake said, casting a contemptuous look up at the sun before closing his eyes and trying to find *her* in the ether.

Mina was in the garage checking on her latest miniature aquarium when she heard the voice of the man who took everything from her in exchange for so much more. When one lived as long as she, it was only natural one developed some hobbies. Her most recent involved traveling to various marshes, creek beds, lakes, and rivers, and collecting mud and water in mason jars to later see what variety of lifeforms she'd managed to rehome. She filmed the results for a somewhat successful YouTube channel and used the ad revenue to pay the bills. In the mason jar before her now, a colony of daphnia shared the muddy water with some snails and a hungry-looking worm.

Drake's voice came to her first as a whisper. As she paid it more heed, it became more tangible and pronounced. His voice had a musicality to it that had captivated her so intensely as a mortal, but now, it only inspired surprise and a little bit of resentment. Once that wore off, he was just another man lucky (or unlucky) enough to gain something close to immortality.

"I thought you were dead," she said.

I'm in California.

"So, you may as well be."

Cute. I . . . we . . . need help.

"Who's we?"

I think you know.

She nearly knocked over a shelf full of mason jar ecosystems in a sudden fit of frustration.

"Don't tell me you're still buddying around with that *devil*."

Can you please just meet us somewhere? The underworld was raided by hunters. It's not safe for us out in the open. We need asylum. Sooner rather than later.

She sat down in a steel chair at her workbench.

"Hunters? Which hunters?"

Harker was leading them. I guess he was still sore about us.

"Was still sore? What do you mean?"

I think he's dead, Mina. I'm sorry.

She steeled her nerves. "No matter. I've not seen him in half a century."

I'm . . . sure it was quick for him.

"I don't want to know," she said, but it was only a half-truth.

Will you help us?

"I don't suppose you know where in California you are. It's a big place, you know."

There was some murmuring. Consulting with Lucifer, no doubt.

We're near an unincorporated locale called Opuntia, do you know it?

The mention of that glorified pitstop made her chew the inside of her right cheek. It was a transitory space, one that she had passed through once in the 1980s while on the run from an overly possessive lover who she'd made the mistake of gifting with the same near-immortality she possessed. Her stop there had resulted in a call so close she had retreated into her own personal exile, one that continued to this day. This was a troubling synchronicity with a past that was distant but not distant enough. She didn't relish going back, but she couldn't just leave Drake out in the open. He had taken death away from her, aside from some very specific causes. For that, she owed him her life.

"I do," she said. "Meet me at a pub called Willie's. You'll have to find transportation to it, though. I've not the time nor the patience to drive all about the desert looking for you two miscreants."

You're the best.

"And don't you forget it."

Never.

And there was something of the old Dracula then in his voice. Before his brides overthrew him and banished him to the underworld. Before he started calling himself Drake and hanging around that no-good fallen angel. It was the voice of the vampire who seduced her, who unmade and remade her.

She glanced at the jars on her shelf. These were essentially self-sustaining ecosystems, requiring minimal nurturing but still oddly important to her. She wanted something or someone to care for, even considering children at one point, though the undead could not give birth and she hadn't the stomach for stealing life from a child. One should have lived some before they gave up their humanity. It needed to be a choice.

She'd been given a choice, *hadn't she?*

Some nights, she wasn't sure. Still, she wouldn't go back to who she was. Not for anything. Harker had been unable to let go, and now he was apparently dead. Sad, but perhaps inevitable.

Mina. Are you there?

"I am."

You'll meet us there? You'll help us?

"I'll see you there, but Drake?"

Yes?

"Don't you or that devil get into any trouble. I'm not one for violence anymore, not unless it's absolutely necessary. I've . . . changed."

A pause. *Of course. See you soon.*

The connection broke. Her surroundings grew less hazy, more concrete. She stood and went looking for her old red dress.

Drake was near the verge of collapse when he glimpsed the sunlight reflecting off the hood of an oncoming vehicle. The glare made him squint, but he blew out a breath of relief.

"I see it," Lucifer said, casting a smug look Drake's way. "I presume you'll need me to do all the talking?"

"Do I look that bad?"

"My friend, you look like shit warmed over."

"You'd know, Devil."

"Just stay out of sight."

Lucifer's hair began to lengthen. The contours of his body shifted, becoming softer and more feminine as the vehicle crested the nearest hill. It was a Cadillac, black and sleek, with tinted windows and a dent in the front bumper.

Drake ducked behind one of the many dunes lining the highway.

The Cadillac slowed as its driver spotted Lucifer who was now fully female and showing a generous amount of leg. The ability to switch between male and female at will was something granted to all angels—fallen or otherwise—and it was something Lucifer used to his advantage as often as he could.

Drake watched as the car stopped and a man climbed out the driver's side door. The guy was middle-aged, paunchy, and going gray. He gave Lady Lucifer a once over. As far as he knew, this was his lucky day.

Were Drake at full power, he would've sprung from his hiding place and ended this right away, but Lucifer reveled in the admiration. He loved hearing this unsuspecting moron's sweet talking. It was all Drake could do not to groan as the driver and Lucifer exchanged pickup lines that ranged from put-on coy cliches to downright vulgar expressions that would've sounded like threats in a different context.

Lucifer twirled her hair like some flirty schoolgirl, and the man put his hands on his hips and leaned in a way to make the bulge in his pants all the more visible. It would've been more amusing if Drake wasn't baking alive out here.

The man gestured to his vehicle, indicating that he aimed to give Lucifer a ride. Before he could say another word, Lucifer's hand lashed out, becoming a fiery blade. The flames encircled the appendage, which now had sharp edges and a jagged point.

Lucifer's arm whooshed as it sliced through the air. The blade's edge cut through the man's neck with the ease of a freshly sharpened circular saw on a thin piece of wood. Much to Drake's dismay, no blood spurted from the wound, as the fire instantly sealed it. The man dropped to his knees, and his head rolled over and off his left shoulder.

Lucifer's hand and body transformed back to the shape Drake

found most familiar. Drake and the devil almost looked like brothers. They were both tall, lithe, and pale, but where Drake's hair was obsidian black, Lucifer sported a head full of blond curls. Drake's eyes matched his hair while Lucifer's blazed like blue fire on a dark night.

Drake rose from behind the dune as his companion approached.

"Men never change," Lucifer said, brushing his hands together as if clearing them of dust. He jerked his thumb toward the car in mockery of the beheaded driver. "Shall we?"

Drake followed Lucifer to the black Cadillac. He made himself walk on his own, despite the exposure having done its damage. He had too much pride to let Lucifer help him stay on his feet, but if he wasn't careful and if he didn't feed soon, he might not have a choice. Night couldn't get here soon enough.

ROSA

Now

ROSA COOK'S FATHER pulled the Ford Explorer alongside one of the pumps at the gas station in Opuntia and cut the engine. Without a word to his wife or daughter, he got out and rushed to the gas station's main structure, a drab, dusty storefront with faded ads for fountain sodas, chili dogs, and lottery tickets in its dirty windows. He threw open the glass door and ran inside, wincing and clutching at his midsection.

Rosa went back to watching skating videos on TikTok.

"Rosa," her mother said.

Rosa waited for the video of a girl doing a midair ollie to finish before looking up. Her mom was eyeing her in the rearview with a sharp but tired gaze.

"Your father . . . " her mother began.

The door to the gas station swung open again. Her father ran out, still holding his belly but instead of heading around back, he bolted for the bar across the gravel lot. His strides were tight and unbalanced as he struggled to not defecate in his pants.

"Out of order!" he hollered so his family could hear him.

Rosa snickered and covered her mouth.

"It's not funny, Rosa," her mother said, though Rosa could see the way her cheeks had flushed pink in the illumination from the dome light, as if she herself were stifling a laugh. "He's had a difficult day. You know that."

"And I'm making it harder," Rosa singsonged.

Her mother sighed. She looked ahead, across the flat land of the California desert at night and toward the mountains to the west. Without her facing Rosa in the rearview, Rosa couldn't read her expression, but she imagined a weary puzzlement there.

70

DRACULA & THE DEVIL WALK INTO A BAR

Something that said, *how did I go wrong? Why is my daughter such a bitch? Though she does have a point about my mother-in-law, may she rest in pieces.*

Or perhaps Rosa was projecting a little.

"I didn't say that," her mother finally said. "Just . . . did you have to walk out on the funeral?"

Rosa slipped her phone into her bag and crossed her arms. "Mom, seriously?"

Her mother turned in the front seat to face her. The dome light was on a timer and now switched off, but she didn't make a move to turn it back on.

"Yes, seriously," she said. "That crossed a line. You know that."

"Sure. Just like I know you wish you would've had the guts to do the same."

This time, there was no hiding it: a laugh did escape her mother's lips. It was a quick one, and she swallowed it before it became something unwieldy, but it was clear and irretrievable. She shook her head and pressed her lips together.

"Your grandmother was a difficult woman."

"A monster," Rosa said. "Those were your words, not mine."

"She could certainly be one, yes, but your father lived with her a long time. Parent-child relationships are complex."

"Yeah, no kidding."

Rosa's mother sighed again and looked in the direction where her husband had run. It was a bar called Willie's. All wood paneling, neon, and corrugated tin. It looked lonely against the desert sky. The mountains beyond resembled sleeping beasts from an age long forgotten.

"Well, there's no telling how long your father's gonna take, and that gas isn't going to pump itself."

"Mhm," Rosa said and reached to take her phone back out. She stopped. "Actually, let me. I'd like to stretch my legs anyway."

Her mother's shoulders relaxed. She handed Rosa the credit card and Rosa got out to refuel the Explorer.

While the digital numbers tracked the dollars and gallons, her mind wandered to the scene at the funeral service. She hadn't wanted to be there to begin with, but when her Uncle Jerry said with a wistful expression on his face that God didn't make women like Gretchen Cook anymore, she had to get out of there before she yelled something offensive, something that couldn't be taken back. If God

71

didn't make women like her grandmother anymore, then the good Lord had finally come to his senses. She excused herself, saying she needed to pee, slipped out of the pew and then out the door.

It was bad enough that she'd left. Much worse that she'd found the preacher's daughter smoking behind the chapel. After sharing the joint, they'd shared some saliva. She let the precocious blonde put a hand down the front of her pants, and that was exactly the compromising position she'd been in at the moment her father came out to find her.

He would never look at her the same way. Sure, he'd always known she was into girls, had even said on numerous occasions that he was cool with it. Seeing it on the day of his mother's funeral, however, was something he could have done without. Now, he couldn't unsee it, and it was likely that the sight just as much as saying a final goodbye to his mother was sending him running to roadside restrooms with a disturbing frequency.

The pump clicked to indicate the tank was full. She replaced the handle and got back into the vehicle. Her father had yet to return. She reached for her phone again but stopped herself and folded her hands.

"You know what really fucks me up about all this?" she asked.

"Language, Rosa."

"Fine. You know what upsets me?" Her mother said nothing. Rosa continued, "You always used to tell me not to let men walk all over you. But then Grandma dies and you're right back at Dad's side, even after what he did."

Her mother's only response was to take a long look at the bar across the lot. She got out and walked around the SUV and slid back in, now in the driver's seat.

"He needs me. I need him. And he didn't walk all over me. He made a bad decision." Rosa scoffed. Her mother added, "You'll understand one day. Now, let's go so we can meet him when he's done."

The engine stirred to life. Rosa felt like screaming.

On the way out of the restroom, Trey Cook stopped to admire the wall of liquors. He could really use a drink after the day he had, but he worried it might further upset his bowels. He spotted a bottle of Basil Hayden's. Maybe it would be worth the risk. He hesitated some more until he saw the woman in red seated at the bar. *Definitely* worth the risk. He wouldn't have time to do anything—not to mention, his nervous guts made him feel anything but sexy—but sometimes simply being in the presence of a gorgeous lady had the power to put his mind at ease.

Fucking hell.

When was he going to get his shit together? Brenda went back to him after he cheated. Maybe it was only to support him while he grieved over his mother and she'd be gone again tomorrow, but he didn't want her to go. He wanted her to stay. And he was going to tell her that he wanted to make things right on the ride back but then Rosa had to get fingered by a preacher's daughter during his mother's funeral and throw a big fat wrench in goddamn *everything*. What a fucked-up day. What a—

"Can I get you something?" the bartender, a man with gray hair and a deeply lined face asked.

Trey swallowed. "Uh, can I get a Basil Hayden's? Neat."

He took a seat at one of the stools, but left plenty of breathing room between himself and the woman in red. A drink was fine, but he wouldn't even look her way. He couldn't rebuild his marriage by laying new cracks.

"God, would you stop fidgeting?" Carmen asked. "You're making me nervous."

"Aren't you the least bit worried?" Derek asked. "He's still not back."

"Don't be such a fucking girl."

"Ugh," Derek said and got up from his table.

Mina overheard the exchange from the two friends of the man she'd killed. She also felt the vibe from the guy who'd just ordered a whiskey and sat a few stools down, heard the disdainful way the lady in the back regarded the returned plate of rare hamburger, and felt the charge of this place on her skin. So many eyes upon her, so many murmured words from other patrons that weren't directly about her but about her just the same. She should not have come here. It was a mistake. Killing the one called Harold should not have happened either, but he'd just looked so damn delicious, and she hadn't tasted freshly shed human blood in an excruciatingly long time.

The one called Derek put his hands on the bar beside her. "Hey," he said.

She didn't even look his way. "Hey."

"So, my friend . . . my cousin. He left with you and didn't come back."

"Mhm," she said and absently drummed her crimson fingertips on the bar.

"So, where is he?" His voice was shakier now, more agitated.

"I'm not sure," she said.

"Well . . . you were the last person to see him, so, uh . . . "

"Listen, Derek," she said, turning to him. His eyes widened, no doubt because she knew his name. "I'm meeting some people here, and they're not gonna want to see me talking to you, so why don't you and your lady friend go back to what you were doing and just accept that Harold checked out for the night because he got hold of something he couldn't handle."

The barely legal boy screwed up his face. "Something he . . . what?"

The woman with him—Carmen—approached and put a hand on his shoulder. "Let's blow this joint. I'm sure Harold's fine. No need to stick around after you already scored, right?" She cast a wink at Mina.

Mina flashed Carmen a saccharine smile. "You should listen to your friend. She's a smart one."

"Fucking bullshit," Derek said. Red bloomed in his cheeks. Thinking of his blood stirred her desire, but she made herself look away. He lingered another couple of seconds like he meant to say more before pushing away from the bar with a huff and turning toward the door.

Mina went back to sitting and waiting, but she could feel the eyes of others on her after the exchange. The group gathered at the pool table had all laid down their sticks. The clearly underage girls playing shuffleboard stared as they sipped their probably spiked sodas.

"Tough crowd," the guy who ordered the whiskey said.

Mina faced him and he grinned.

"Don't fucking start," she said.

He put up his hands in a *don't shoot* gesture, then returned to his drink. Drake and Lucifer couldn't get here soon enough.

Where are those godforsaken jerks?

When Lucifer waved his hand over the hole containing the two dead men, the corpses went up in flames. The bloody sheets and pieces of plywood from the makeshift shelter where they'd found the man with the slashed throat caught and burned too.

"And to think she told us not to get into any trouble," he said with a light laugh. "Both these bodies are her fault."

Drake averted his eyes from the fire. The desert was a black expanse around them, broken only by scattered lights from open businesses and the neighborhood across the highway. The blood of the man from the store pulsed beneath his skin, only stoking his appetite for more after so much time underground, so much time *dormant*. It wasn't simply food he craved; it was the rush, the thrill of the kill. His heart thumped twice as hard as it had in decades.

"I mean," Lucifer continued, "sure, we killed the poor gas station clerk, but we wouldn't have had to if he hadn't found—"

"Will you stop talking?" Drake hissed through his teeth.

Lucifer cocked an eyebrow. "Feeling testy, are we?"

"A bit."

The bodies crackled and popped in the dancing flames. Sparks and smoke drifted up from the hole, and the stink of burning flesh made Drake's head swoon with memories of the day his castle was razed by those treacherous, ungrateful whores he'd gifted with near immortality. Mina wasn't like them, though. Mina was better—still willing to help after he spent so many years away, so loyal, so faithful. This reunion was a long time coming.

"I understand," Lucifer said. "Love of your life . . . "

"Of many lifetimes."

" . . . and you're worried she's changed in the time you've been away."

Drake said nothing.

"Well, worry not. As I said, these corpses are her doing, though only one directly so."

"Can't those bodies burn any faster?" Drake asked.

Lucifer raised his hands and curled his fingers. The red flames shifted in tone from orange to blue and then to white. In their glow, the devil's smile was all too plain to see. With the bodies fully incinerated, the fire died down, leaving Drake and Lucifer in a more perfect darkness.

"Let's go meet your little lady," Lucifer said.

They faced the neon-adorned, tin-roofed structure of Willie's Tavern just as an SUV pulled up in front of it. Its lower panels and the tires were dusty from the day's travels. Drake could tell there were two women inside—one older and one younger, perhaps a mother and daughter. His tongue tingled with the stirrings of his reawakened, insatiable thirst.

Rosa's mother turned in the front seat to face her daughter in the back.

"Wait here," she said in a stern but tired voice.

"Fuck that," Rosa said, and opened her door.

"Rosa!" her mother called, but Rosa had already stepped out into the desert night and shut the door. Her mother went out after her, catching up on the front steps of the old-school, wood-paneled tavern. "Just wait up, okay?"

Rosa took hold of the tavern door and held it open for her mother. With a gesture, she ushered her mother forward. A man and a woman tromped out, nearly pushing past Rosa and her mother. The woman was tall and broad-shouldered. The man was scrawny and short. His cheeks blazed red with either frustration or embarrassment.

"Watch it," the woman said, practically spitting it.

The man walked behind her with his head bowed low.

Rosa got a bad feeling about going into this bar, but nevertheless, she stepped through its barn-style door. It was Rosa's first time inside such an establishment. Once inside, she was met with an array of sounds and smells that let her know she was out of her element. Crunchy dad rock played over the PA, something by AC/DC or someone like that—she could never tell the old bands apart. The odor of spilled beer mingled with the stench of stale nicotine. A feeling she didn't belong overtook her as soon as the door shut behind her. The place felt alien, grownup, *dangerous*. She nearly spun and went back outside, but she spotted her dad— and the beauty seated a couple seats away. The woman turned to face Rosa, as Rosa's mother crossed the bar to approach her father.

Rosa hardly noted her parents' actions. The woman's gaze had a hypnotic effect. She was more than simply striking, mature, and zeroed in on Rosa. She was also strangely familiar. Rosa felt that she'd seen this woman before but also knew that was impossible. Could it have been a dream? Or another life? That was absurd! And yet—

"What the hell are you doing getting a drink?" Rosa's mother asked in an exasperated tone.

The sudden outburst drew Rosa's attention, but the woman lingered in her periphery like a sentient shadow in a child's room at night.

"Harold!" Derek hollered. He and Carmen had just found Harold's pickup, still parked in front of Willie's. Derek stepped into the center of the lot. This was all wrong. He cupped his hands around his mouth. "Harold!"

"He's probably around back," Carmen said, stomping around the building to check.

"You don't sound so fucking sure of yourself!"

Carmen glared over her shoulder. "Watch your mouth, boy. Or I'll give you a beating that will make you wish you never came back to this town."

"This isn't a town," Derek muttered and absently yanked on the truck's door handle. It didn't give, not like he had expected it would. This whole thing was weird. He was about to suggest they call the police, but awareness of something else drew his attention. "Hey, do you smell that? It smells like . . . "

He was going to say barbecued pork, but there was nothing suspicious about that. Plus, it didn't exactly smell like that; it smelled stronger, headier.

What is that?

"Oh, what the fuck?" Carmen said from behind the tavern.

"Carmen?" Derek pushed away from the vehicle and began heading her way. He moved at a trot, a sense of urgency adding a spring to his steps. He found Carmen behind the building standing over a mattress laid between some oil barrels. Shards of plastic and shreds of wire littered the ground around it. He scrunched up his face. "What is this?"

"It's where he takes them," Carmen said, as if it should be obvious.

"Them?" Derek asked.

Carmen blew out an exaggerated sigh. "The ladies he picks up, stupid."

Derek gave the drab surroundings another once over. "Here?"

"Oh, and I suppose you take the ladies to the Ritz?" Carmen put her hands on her hips and stood up straight. "There are usually sheets and stuff on the bed, at least. And a radio. Where the fuck is he?" She turned and started. "Oh. Well, hello, handsome. Make that *handsomes.*"

Derek followed her gaze to see two slender pretty boys, one dark-haired, the other blond. The dark-haired guy wore black pants and a black coat with a blood-red shirt. The blond wore all white and had eyes like sky-colored jewels. They looked like brothers, but as if they each came from different realities—one of fire, one of shadow.

"Where's my cousin?" Derek said, finding his words and remembering his liquid courage.

"These guys don't know," Carmen said. She got closer to them. "Do you fellas?"

"Actually," the blond said, "him and the gas station man were just incinerated in a hole out yonder."

Carmen's face twisted into something like a dog's angry snarl. But before she could spit a single syllable, the dark-haired man's torso transformed. Chest and stomach muscles bulged, becoming ropey, tumorous protrusions. The shirt he wore ripped apart and fell off him in rags. His hands became claws, shedding their fingernails to make room for yellow, jagged talons. Leathery membranes stretched from beneath his arms with sickening ripping sounds; they looked like wings. His face contorted: eyes flashing to red, nose becoming a snout, fangs sprouting from his jaws.

"What the actual fuck?" Derek spat.

The bat creature opened its mouth impossibly wide and closed over the top of Carmen's head. She screamed as her skull crunched beneath the monster's jaws. Blood gushed down the lower half of her face and soaked the front of her blouse. The creature pulled its head up, taking everything above Carmen's cheekbones with it. The blood shot up in geysers from the ragged hole as Carmen dropped to her knees, then crumpled over in a heap. Her hands clawed at the sand—hands that didn't get the memo that their host was dead.

Something warm spread at the front of Derek's pants as he watched the bat creature chew on Carmen's brains and crunch shards of her skull. Piss. It was fucking piss, but he was too terrified to feel ashamed. Nor did he have the time. He needed to get out of here lest he suffer the same fate.

He sprang to the side, going from stationary to sprint in a split second.

But it wasn't fast enough.

"Ah-ah," the blond one said.

Over the frantic thuds of his footsteps, Derek heard the sound of snapping fingers. An instant later, fire engulfed his skin.

"What the hell is going on out there?" the man behind the bar asked.

Mina knew the answer and knew it wasn't good. A silence had fallen over the tavern after the successive screams from outside. Only the music on the juke kept playing, but even that sounded muted. The air was thick with the palpable sense that something terrible was about to happen—that something terrible already had, and something worse would follow.

She never should've agreed to come here. Drake and Lucifer together always brought out the worst in each other. They always tried to outdo one another when it came to killing. Who could make a bigger mess? Who could do it cleaner? Who could kill the most? Who could kill one specific target first? There was no end to it. She was a fool to think this would have somehow changed after a few decades in hiding. The worst part about those two was once the killing started, it was nearly impossible to stop it. Of course, she was no saint, she thought, remembering the throat she'd slit and subsequently drank from out back. But perhaps she could stop it all now by simply leaving. Break the cycle. Go back to her jars. Leave Drake and Lucifer stranded.

She stood up and stopped. That *girl* was still standing in front of the door, now appearing all the more vulnerable that her mother had left her side and those screams had torn through the desert night air. Mina could not leave this girl to die in whatever wave of carnage was about to come through Willie's Tavern tonight.

"Get away from the door," she hissed at the girl.

The girl blinked and briskly walked to her parents. The father put his hand on her shoulder, and she didn't pull away.

"Do you know something about this?"

The inquiry came from behind the bar, not from the bartender, but the cook. She was staring hard at Mina with eyes like black stones, and not just because Mina sent back the burger she'd made. The other patrons spoke amongst themselves in hushed whispers. Above the muted din, Mina could hear two sets of footsteps outside. She faced the bartender who wore a stupid, slack-jawed expression that made Mina want to scream.

"If there's a back door, I suggest you and everyone else go out it now," she said, doing everything she could to keep her tone even.

"What is this?" the bartender asked.

Mina bared her teeth. "*Now!*"

The footsteps outside came to a halt. No one on the inside moved. The latch on the tavern's front entrance clicked, and the door eased open. Mina stepped into the center of the tavern floor, waiting to meet her fate and preserve the fates of everyone else inside.

MINA AND ROSA

POWER, ROSA THOUGHT. That was what the woman in red possessed. It was all in how she stood, legs apart, shoulders back, face stoic. Her hands made closed fists. She looked ready to meet whatever horror came through that door. Meet it and knock it back. She was an immovable object and there was no force too irresistible.

"Mom, Dad," Rosa whispered. "I think we should do what she says."

The door swung all the way open, and two men stepped through. They had an otherworldly quality about them, similar to that of the woman in red but something far more menacing— perhaps that was due to them coming inside so soon after the screams. One of the men was delicately featured, *pretty* almost, and dressed in white clothes. The other was nude above the waist and something dark glistened around his mouth and nose. It looked like—

"Shit, is that blood?" the bartender asked.

The shirtless man wiped his mouth absently, then looked down at his hands. Something twinkled in his eyes, something too good-humored given the circumstances.

"It sure looks like it," the man said and grinned.

"Drake," the woman in red said. There was a slight waver to her voice, almost too slight to detect, but Rosa felt an uncanny bond with this woman, one that made her think no one else, except maybe the two newcomers, detected it.

Drake licked the blood from his fingers and grinned wider. The man in white laughed as he scanned his surroundings, taking stock of everyone inside the establishment. The laugh was a strangely musical sound. He stopped laughing and stopped looking around when his eyes met Rosa's. Those pale blues brightened at the sight of her.

"Well, now," he said. "This just became a party."

One of the men from the pool tables squared up to Drake and the man in white. He white-knuckled his pool cue, ready to use it if the situation so required. He wore a dirty T-shirt that barely contained his grizzly bear frame, faded blue jeans, and steel-toe boots. His jaw muscles clenched as he fixed the two newcomers with a hard stare. He softened a little when he looked at the lady in red. Rosa heard his words before he said them.

"Are these guys bothering you?" he asked predictably.

"I've got it under control, thanks." The reply came through gritted teeth.

Not taking a hint, the would-be white knight stood in front of her and faced the two men. He raised the pool cue like a samurai sword. Drake and the man in white exchange a glance. What happened next was something Rosa never would have thought possible in real life. Drake grabbed hold of the man's arms and positioned him with his back toward the man in white. The man in white's right hand disappeared in a flash of orange, replaced by something resembling a fiery sword. The man in white drove the blade into the back of the man with the pool cue. It went all the way through his considerable torso, the tip bursting through his chest cavity like a pickaxe through ice. It remained engulfed in flames, spilling no blood but causing pungent smoke to emit from the wound and the man's screaming mouth. With uncanny strength, Drake yanked the man's arms, and they came free with twin sickening rips and pops. Blood spurted from the shoulder stumps and Drake held the arms over his head, drizzling blood onto his face and wagging his tongue to ensure he caught every drop.

It was now apparent what had caused the screams outside. Now, everyone inside Willie's Tavern was screaming too.

When the man called Drake and the man in white first entered, Leonard Torres thought again about Art History. The masculine but delicate contours of the man in white's face called to mind something classically sculpted, either from the Renaissance or Ancient Greece. Drake exuded pure Dark Romanticism. In the wake of the bloody confrontation with poor Hal Goodman—who'd simply been trying to see if the woman in red needed help—the scene resembled no art movement he could recall from his college days. Even if he by some miracle had kept his notes from back then, he was reasonably sure he'd studied nothing so grotesque or violent. This was something out of a horror movie or a recreation of a scene from hell itself.

Hal was still screaming. Smoke billowed from his mouth and the wound in his chest. Crimson spurted from his shoulder stumps to the rhythm of his frantic heartbeat. This was beyond cruel and vile, Leonard thought. The man had grandkids, for God's sake. Leonard remembered the shotgun he kept behind the bar under the register. He reached for it now.

Hal stopped screaming, but all around, others were crying and whimpering. Two of the girls at the shuffleboard table cowered underneath the table, their sodas now icy lakes at their feet. The third scrambled toward the bar and tried to climb over. The family that had come in was trying to do likewise, clambering around the counter as the two killers remained focused on the dying Hal. The woman in red was screaming something at Drake that Leonard couldn't make out. He recalled her earlier warning.

If there's a back door, I suggest you and everyone else go out it now.

So, she knew these two. What did she have to do with all this? Leonard had known she was trouble and had feared that trouble would follow her in here. He hadn't expected something like this, though. This was beyond expectations.

Hal's body stopped jerking. The blood spurts lessened in frequency. Drake dropped the arms like a couple of floppy dumbbells, and the man in white retracted his fiery blade. Before Hal crumpled to the floor, the blade was a hand again.

Leonard pulled the shotgun from under the counter and leveled it at the man in white. He didn't care what sort of supernatural abilities the man apparently possessed; buckshot was buckshot, and no one stood up to it, not at this range. He racked and fired.

It was a good shot, most of the projectiles catching Leonard's target in the chest and shoulder area. The force knocked the man in white backwards and into the nearest window. The glass shattered, spilling large, jagged shards to the floor, and the man in white sailed to the outside.

Drake and the woman in red faced Leonard with an expression that wasn't quite surprise. He racked the gun again and pointed it at Drake.

"Suck this, motherfucker!" he shrieked, not caring that he sounded less like an action hero and more like a severely distressed preschooler.

The second shotgun blast missed its mark, instead shattering a window beside Drake. The killer didn't waste a second in the wake of the shot. He sprang, leaping onto the counter. When his feet struck the bar top, his torso changed, rippling and bulging. His face twisted and stretched. Arms became wings.

Leonard leveled the shotgun, sure he couldn't miss at this range, but Drake—or whatever Drake had become—was simply too quick. He buried his snout into the space where Leonard's neck met his left shoulder and ripped free a hunk of bloody gristle. The pain was enough to make Leonard drop the weapon. A second bite tore another piece of his neck free, and as he slumped to the floor behind the bar, he saw the man in white inexplicably climbing back inside. The man showed no apparent signs he'd been shot. No wounds whatsoever on his sculpted torso. Even the clothes were somehow still intact. And it was this final impossible image in a sequence of impossible images that sent Leonard plunging into the abyss of unconsciousness, and finally, into death.

"Now, *that* hurt," Lucifer said. "Almost forgot what that feels like. Getting shot, I mean."

Drake stepped down from the bar counter. Human-shaped again, he licked the blood from his lips. A tough shred of gristle had lodged itself into his teeth and he prodded at it with his tongue. The family and one of the girls from the shuffleboard table had made it into the back with the cook, but they wouldn't escape. Lucifer had seen to that by sealing the back door with a hex. It was a temporary seal, but they wouldn't need a lot of time to dispose of every living thing in this tavern. As a matter of fact—

"How long do you think, Lucifer? How fast do you wager we can make this place a slaughterhouse?"

"Drake, this isn't necessary," Mina said. "It's already a slaughterhouse. Let's just leave."

One of the remaining men from the pool tables charged forward with a triumphant grunt. He had broken down his pool cue and was holding both pieces together to form a makeshift cross, like some blue-collar Peter Cushing. Drake always hated those movies.

"Back, demons!" he yelled, shifting the cross's focus from Drake to Lucifer to Mina. "In the name of God, get back!"

The man's eyes were wide and filled with Pentecostal fervor. His teeth were bared like a mad dog's and the cords in his neck all stood out. He was a squat man, no more than five and a half feet tall, but what he lacked in height, he more than made up for in girth. His arms were like thick snakes, bulging and ropey. His legs were as thick as telephone poles. A beer belly peeped out from beneath a shirt that said MUST BE THIS TALL TO RIDE over a line painted across the shirt's middle, which would make any potential "riders" just a little over four feet tall. He had a knife clipped to his belt, but clearly, his faith lay in iconography instead of weaponry. Not like either would do him any good here, not unless that knife was made of silver.

"Get back, demons!" he cried. "Get behind me, Satan!"

Lucifer sighed. He pointed with his thumb and index finger to mimic a gun. He flicked down the thumb and a fiery projectile not unlike one of Cupid's mythical arrows shot across the room. It caught Cushing in the throat, leaving a charred, smoldering hole in place of his Adam's apple. Cushing and the two pieces of pool cue hit the floor. He clutched at the wound and gurgled, but he was good as dead.

The two women under the shuffleboard table made for the door. Lucifer's left hand shot out, becoming a massive pole of fire.

"Ah-ah-ah, ladies," he said. "And Drake, you were wondering how long it will take to kill everyone in this joint? I bet we can do it in under three minutes."

The two girls cowered and cried out, alternating between curses and pleas. Mina grabbed Lucifer by the right arm and heaved him away from the door. His left hand returned to one of flesh as he slammed against the bar.

"No killing kids," Mina said. The two girls ran screaming into the night. Lucifer looked to the remaining men from the pool tables. One was backed into a corner, holding a handgun in a trembling grip. The other stood between two tables with a dark stain of urine across the front of his pants. "Or anyone else," Mina said. "Let's just *go*."

Lucifer faced Drake. The former Count had a decision to make. All the blood he'd consumed thrummed through him. He could hardly recall the last time he felt so alive. Every capillary hummed with vitality. His pulse pounded in his head with the sheer exhilaration of feeding and spreading carnage. Lucifer met his gaze with eyes full of life, and Drake knew his companion from the underworld felt the same way. There was thrill in the kill. In chaos. In blood and fire.

But then there was Mina. She had so gracefully agreed to meet them, to provide them asylum, even after he had left her topside, remaining with Lucifer in the underworld long after the heat from the revolt of his brides had died down. Lucifer had been more than a brother, but—

Don't you or that devil get into any trouble. I'm not one for violence anymore, not unless it's absolutely necessary. I've . . . changed.

Had she? She started this . . .

But maybe we're taking it too far. Maybe she's right.

Drake looked from her to Lucifer. He loved them both dearly. Lucifer had given him a home when he had none. Accepted him when the world rejected him because Lucifer himself knew what it was like to be rejected. Violent or non-violent, a seducer or simply seductive, he never had to worry about Lucifer judging him or putting limitations on him. They were pure chaos together, a literal match made in hell. They committed so much mayhem together and had so much fun doing it. Letting those dark impulses take over, not keeping them in some cage, neglected and building until they grew unwieldy. Or perhaps Mina was right: simply giving into these violent urges made them unwieldy. At least in the underworld, actions didn't matter so much. Life had no meaning there because there was no death. But here . . .

He held Mina's gaze, saw the pure love in her eyes. Like Lucifer's love, it was unconditional, but it also came with boundaries—boundaries set out of love. Boundaries that if he were to go on living, not looking over his shoulder at every turn, he would need. He opened his mouth to tell Mina, *yes, no more killing*, then, *come on, Lucifer, let's go*. He opened his mouth, but the words did not emerge. They were not given the chance.

DRACULA & THE DEVIL WALK INTO A BAR

A barrage of heavy projectiles blasted him off his feet, sending him flying over the bar and crashing into the wall of liquor bottles. He tried to peer over the top of the bar and see who had attacked him, but his shredded, agony-wracked body was too weak to move beyond coughing up blood and gasping for air. The damn bullets were made of silver. He only saw the outline of his assailant for a brief moment. It was enough time to realize who it was, but not enough to speak or even think the bastard's name.

A life that had lasted five hundred and a half years ended in a blink.

The bullets that ended Drake didn't take one life. The shooter had been careless or indiscriminate or some combination of the two. The projectiles had blown into the kitchen area where Rosa had been hiding with her parents, the cook, and the remaining girl at the shuffleboard table after they'd learned they couldn't open the back door. The cook's head exploded when hit, showering the kitchen and the others in hunks of brain and slivers of skull. The last shuffleboard girl caught a bullet to the midsection, cutting her in two. Both sections of her body plopped to the floor, lifeless but gooey with blood and gore. A third of the massive projectiles had taken the arm of Rosa's father. He collapsed into her mother, just as a fourth bullet pierced them both. They fell into a final embrace. Only Rosa remained—covered in blood amidst all the tragic collateral damage. She tried not to weep, not out of pride, but because she didn't want to risk being found.

Harker, very much alive in spite of any mishaps during his raid on the underworld, stood in the doorframe of Willie's tavern surveying the bullet-riddled corpse of Count Dracula.

Mina could hardly believe the sight before her. While true that she had undergone a variety of changes over the past century, Harker's changes were far more overt.

She hardly recognized him.

While his face had retained its familiar angles, it now housed red eyes and jagged metal teeth. The redness was artificial, not attained by vampirism or any sort of demonic energy. The most dramatic transformations, however, happened below the face. His torso was grotesquely enlarged, with metal plates hammered into his flesh. His arms had been replaced, one by a minigun, the other by a chainsaw and what looked like a blowtorch. His legs, like his torso, were bloated and augmented with metal plates.

"Jonathan," she breathed.

God, what a colossally fucked-up day.

The two remaining men by the pool tables tried to book it for the door. Harker swung the chainsaw, severing one head, then another. Both heads dropped to the ground and rolled, eyes staring accusatorily at Mina in their last living moments. The headless bodies took a couple more steps before smacking into each other and crashing out yet another window, spilling jagged shards of glass. Harker then set his sights on Lucifer.

"Oh, well, heh . . . " Lucifer began, trying to play nonchalant, devil-may-care, but he'd always been quick to remind others he wasn't the devil, and it showed now as grief and rage twisted his features into the monstrous thing the world had always said he was. Curved horns tore through the flesh of his forehead, each growing to nearly three feet long. His teeth extended and sharpened to points. Literal fire filled his eyes, engulfed his fists, and fanned out as colossal wings from his back. "*YOU FUCKING BASTARD! I'LL GODDAMN END YOU!*"

Harker pointed the blowtorch, but instead of fire, it emitted a thick blue mist. The mist swirled around Lucifer, enshrouding him completely, stifling his cries and dimming his flames. When it cleared, the Morning Star was frozen in a large block of ice, silently screaming behind a blue-white barrier, his eyes pulled wide with terror and rage, his hands making fists that would never strike or become swords again. Every lick of fire had gone out. He was dead—or as close to death as a fallen angel could get.

Mina met the now-mechanical gaze of the man to whom she was once engaged. That was nearly two lifetimes ago. Two lifetimes and multiple transformations. Yet, there was something left of her fiancé in this cyborg. She could tell in how he looked at her, in how he had travelled to the underworld to avenge her loss, and in how she felt now in his presence. She had loved him then, and she loved him now. It was inexplicable, she thought as she examined the mayhem around her, but *love* was inexplicable.

He held out his arms. The barrels of the minigun were still smoking, but the chainsaw had gone quiet. He stared at her, and though it was impossible given his augmented features, she thought she saw an expectant expression in his eyes. She cast another glance at the ruined corpse of the once enigmatic Count and stepped into the cyborg's embrace.

Even the fleshy parts of his body were cold. She doubted if he even still had blood pumping through his veins. No, likely only battery power and scornful rage had kept him alive. Could love for her sustain him the way those things had? Could *she* love him enough to give him back his soul? Did she want to?

She pressed harder against him. The metal limbs were hard and cold against her skin, but perhaps she could come to appreciate the feeling. If that was what she wanted.

Something occurred to her. She reached behind his neck, feigning affection but feeling for something vital, like a wire or a joint. When she found what she was looking for, she closed her hand around it.

"How did you find us?" she asked. Unless he had followed Drake and Lucifer from the moment they escaped the underworld, there was only one other feasible way. Harker didn't answer. She pulled away slightly so she could meet his gaze, but she kept her hand around the cable at the back of his neck. "How?"

"I did what needed to be done." His voice crackled with static.

"The Hezekian Ritual?" Harker offered no response. Mina breathed deep and asked more pointedly. "Did you murder a child so you could find where Dracula had escaped to?"

"Mina . . . " Harker began, but she decided she didn't want to hear whatever it was he had to say because she already knew what the answer would be. She tightened her grip around the cable plugged into the base of his skull and gave it a fierce tug. It ripped loose with a burst of sparks and sizzle. The red eyes blinked to black, came back to red once, then died for good. Mina stepped back as the bulky mass of metal and flesh slumped and fell forward.

She expected to cry, standing over the corpses of two men she'd loved and amidst so much death in general, but her eyes were dry as the sand in the surrounding desert. It wasn't because she now realized she didn't love them, and it wasn't because she thought she wouldn't cry sometime later. Instead, it was simpler than that. Mina was, in every way, unfathomably exhausted. She turned toward the kitchen, where she heard the frantic hammering of a young and wounded heart.

Rosa didn't know how long she remained huddled on the kitchen floor. She was shuddering with a combination of adrenaline and cold from being soaked with blood in the conditioned air. She had her knees hugged to her chest, and try as she might, she couldn't rip her gaze away from the entangled corpses of her parents. They'd died in each other's arms.

It should've been poetic—a lover's death, in spite of the recent turmoil in their marriage. The grotesque nature of the wounds rendered the scene void of anything other than horror.

Rosa continued to stare, knowing full well that the macabre image would be imprinted on her mind for the rest of her life. It would be imprinted there even if she stopped staring now, but she kept staring. She couldn't tell herself why, only she kept getting this vague notion that they might get up and laugh, maybe take a bow, and then pull her in for a full-family embrace like this was some absurd joke and not at all in poor taste.

None of this happened, but the notion remained.

Approaching footsteps drew her gaze. At the sight of the woman in red, Rosa scrambled to her feet, but skidded on the blood and fell promptly back to her ass. Her hands thrashed about, trying to find something to use as a weapon. All she managed to find was a cooking tray, which she held up as a pathetic excuse for a shield. The woman in red stood over her but made no move to attack.

"Wh-who are you?" she shrieked. "What the fuck was all that?"

Her hands trembled, but she maintained her white-knuckle grip on the tray.

"I'm Mina," the woman said. "I'm a friend."

"Bullshit," Rosa said through quavering lips.

"Right. You don't know me, but I won't hurt you."

Rosa looked to the bodies of her parents. Her bottom lip trembled.

"Your mother and father," Mina said. "I'm sorry for your losses. I've had my own share today. To be completely truthful, I feel partially responsible, but I'm . . . I'd like to make amends."

"How? How could you possibly hope to do that?"

"I can take you away from all this." Mina gestured to the smoking, bloody mess around them. "Give you a new life."

Rosa scoffed and wiped a strand of blood that had found its way to her lips. She still hadn't lowered the tray. She refused, even though she knew it would do little to protect her. She needed to have something, some sense of security, even a false one.

"I mean it," Mina said. "It won't be immortality, but it will be close enough. If we lay low, we won't be hunted down."

Rosa looked up at the woman. She hoped her expression showed the disdain she so profoundly felt.

"You're asking if I want to be made into a vampire?"

"I am. Being a vampire doesn't need to mean being a monster. You can live off of meat served rare. At night, you can do things you never thought possible, such as fly and transform into—"

"Bats and wolves?"

"And more if you so desire. Drake—Dracula—first appeared to me as swirling fog that seeped through the window of my chambers. That was one-hundred and thirty—"

"Wait, *the* Dracula? You're *that* Mina?" Mina gave Rosa a slow nod. Rosa exhaled and pressed her hands to her eyes. "Oh, God, this can't be real."

"I wish in many ways that it wasn't," Mina said. "But since that isn't possible, we can only make the most of it. Police will be here soon, I imagine. I also imagine you don't want to go with them, and wind up shuffled from foster home to foster home for the next— what, three years until you turn eighteen."

"Give or take," Rosa said, now suddenly shifty. "And no, that doesn't sound ideal at all."

"Then, come with me," Mina said. "Let me raise you as my own."

Rosa stood and lowered the tray but didn't drop it just yet. "Will it . . . hurt?"

"At first, but then—"

"Yeah, I figured that was a given. So, how does this work? You bite me and then I drink from you?"

"Yes."

"And no more killing?"

"No more killing."

"Okay," Rosa said, nodding slowly. There were sirens now, and they weren't far away by the sounds of them. She tossed the tray aside, stepped toward Mina and held out her arms. "Okay, let's do it."

Mina pulled her into an embrace. The woman in red's lips were cool against her neck, the inside of her mouth was warm. When the teeth entered, Rosa cried out. It did hurt, but it wasn't entirely unpleasant. She felt a brief panic as her life force began to drain from her, and she clawed frantically at Mina's arms. Mina stroked the back of Rosa's head; it had a calming effect as Mina continued to drink. The sirens had to be closer now, but they sounded even farther away. Blackness closed over her, and it was the most peace she felt all day.

EPILOGUE

ROSA AWOKE ON a futon in a room full of mason jars and terrariums. The glass containers were filled with a wide variety of foliage. In some of them, she could see tiny creatures moving about. The woman in red—Mina—was seated in a chair looking over her. She was no longer wearing the red dress, but a gray tank top and black yoga pants. She looked like an average suburban mom, which struck Rosa as funny considering this woman was a century-and-a-half-old vampire.

Rosa felt different. She wasn't groggy like she normally was when she woke. Her muscles felt stronger, well-nourished. She was also hyper-aware, could hear things outside that she shouldn't be able to hear, passing conversations, dog paws padding on the sidewalk. Despite this increased power of her senses, she never felt overwhelmed or anxious. There was no sensory overload.

"It worked, didn't it?" she asked, but she already knew the answer.

Mina simply smiled. Her eyes held a serenity Rosa seldom saw in anyone. It was the expression of a woman who'd been through hell, but had lived through it, emerged from its flames ready to *truly* live.

Rosa took Mina's hand and squeezed it. Something tickled her frontal lobe. The memory of her parents in their terminal embrace surfaced. It didn't come with the pain she expected because she knew that *their* pain was gone. She knew it more than she could have known through any human faith or scientific explanation. Her newfound near-immortality had apparently come with transcendent wisdom.

She would miss them, though—she already did—but she also knew on a fundamental level that suffering, not death, was the true evil, the true cause for grief, and her parents would suffer no more.

Now, she had a new life to live, one free from her old one, and if she was careful, one free from the endless cycle of death and suffering faced by mortals.

She hoped she wouldn't get bored.

"So, what now?" she asked, frowning up at the woman who'd taken everything from her but given her so much more.

Mina's smile only broadened. She gestured to the wall of terrariums. "Want to see what I've been working on?"

"Sure," Rosa said with a slight chuckle. "Why not?"

She got to her feet and watched as Mina took down a mason jar with small but vibrant green leaves carpeting its rocky substrate. Mina set the jar on an end table and switched on a lamp overhead. Rosa bent to get a closer look. There was an entire world inside the tiny jar, a self-sustaining ecosystem contained within glass. She could get lost looking inside it for days, and why not? She had all the time in the world.

ROAD WRATH

CARVER PIKE

CHAPTER 1

"SLOW DOWN! You're gonna drive us off the side of the mountain!"

Her high-pitched squeal made Doug cringe. Yesterday, he would have described Honey's voice as the sweetest damn thing he'd ever heard. It was the voice he craved at night and loved waking up to in the morning.

Now, it reminded him of one of his wife's cats in heat – his wife's cats because he'd never wanted the damned things in the first place. Although he'd never hit a woman in his life, he was filled with the sudden urge to backhand Honey if she didn't stop barking orders at him. It was hard enough to concentrate without her yowling from the passenger seat.

They were on the run. From what, he didn't know, but he'd seen the damage it could do and knew if it caught them, they were dead.

"Please," she begged, "we're gonna flip off the road if you keep taking turns like that."

"Did you not see what it did to Meg?"

She'd seen. They all had. They'd been setting up their tents, about to start a long weekend of drinking and fucking. Doug and his brother, Stan, had both been excited about this camping trip alone with their 'booty calls.' It was the first time they'd brought the women together. Doug was married, so Honey was his secret side chick while Meg was simply one of Stan's 31 flavors.

At forty-five and having been divorced twice already, Stan was in no rush to tie the knot again. He cycled through girlfriends the way most guys did outfits. He often joked about Doug's situation and used it as a prime example of why he'd never get hitched again.

"Little brother," he'd recently said, "look at you. You've got a woman at home who nags at you all the time and spends all your money. Then you've got this fine piece of ass you clearly enjoy spending time with who never bitches or complains, still does quite a bit of spending I should probably add, but lives to have a good time in and out of bed. I've been where you are already. It's how I met my second wife, Ariel, and I guarantee you, if you were to drop Bev and marry Honey, Honey would become Bev within a year's time. Then you'd be looking for a new Honey."

Stan was right. He'd known that, but still, Honey hinted at marriage all the time. Usually, it was after sex while lying in bed together. When she played with his balls or stroked him and tried to get him ready for a second round of lovemaking, she'd bring up how great it would be if they were married and how much sex they could really have then. She never mentioned him divorcing Bev, but one couldn't happen without the other.

Several times, he'd considered calling things off with Honey. He'd tried to do it face-to-face because over the phone seemed wrong, but she'd always show up in a short skirt and a shirt that showed too much cleavage. Next thing, he'd have her bent over someplace, fucking promises into her he'd had no intention of keeping.

Right now was the first time they'd been put in a pressure situation together, and he knew without a doubt, if they made it out alive, he was going to tell her to take a hike.

He couldn't fucking stand her anymore. It was taking everything in his power not to kick her out the passenger door.

"Doug," Honey said, "slow the fuck down."

"Shut the fuck up," came his response.

His foot punched the gas pedal instead of the brake. Slowing down was not an option. He needed to go faster because he knew nothing about the thing that was following them except that it was fast, strong, and ferocious.

They'd finished setting up camp and were sitting in a circle, pouring shots, when Meg slipped off to pee. She hadn't gone far because she was afraid of the dark and of bears. She couldn't have been gone a full minute when she came rushing toward the circle in her hot pink sweatsuit.

She was a dainty thing. Cute and petite with a strawberry blonde bob and a sprinkling of freckles across the bridge of her nose and cheeks. She might have been in her early thirties but looked younger.

"Guys," she'd said nervously. "There's something out there."

"There's lots of things out there," Stan had replied sarcastically. "It's fuckin' Appalachia, babe."

Doug was taking a hit from the bong and laughing his ass off. With his eyes on Honey, he saw her face change from amusement to pure terror. Her forehead creased, her eyes opened wide, and her mouth opened to yell, but no words came out.

As he looked at Meg, he saw his brother trip over the beer cooler and fall on his ass.

Nobody could make sense of the shadowy creature much wider than Meg's tiny body. Its face was hidden behind her, but its dark, hairy, enormous legs and arms unraveled from their tucked-in position.

Meg whimpered, seeming to suddenly understand that the thing she'd warned them about was behind her.

Before she could react, the creature's hand punched straight through her gut.

Blood splattered the ground.

Clawed fingernails opened wide in front of Meg's stomach and turned around so its palm was facing upward as the massive hand opened and closed. Then it snapped shut over her chest from the outside and lifted her body straight up into the air.

Meg's face twisted into a look of pure agony and terror. Her mouth stretched open wide over her teeth and her eyes went bloodshot, twitching in their sockets, while a blend of blood and drool dripped down from the corners of her mouth and over her chin before pooling at her feet.

"Wha . . . hel . . . help me," she'd squeaked like a child who didn't understand why she was being punished.

The black, clawed hand sticking out the front of her chest opened and closed again. Blood dripped from its jagged fingernails. Meg's face fell forward, and she gurgled before hissing out her final breath. Her body crumpled into a heap on the ground. Doug and the others ran.

"What the fuck was that?" Stan yelled as they raced through the woods, heading for their cars.

Honey, who was clenching Doug's hand, only cried.

Doug kept repeating, "What the fuck? What the fuck? What the fuck?"

It seemed unreal.

They'd just lit the fire and were about to cook hotdogs. Stan was in the middle of pulling beers from the icy cooler. They'd only started to hit the bong. Meg hadn't even taken her turn.

Now, Meg was dead.

Stan was in the car behind them as they sped through the rain, zipped along I-79's straight aways, and hauled ass around the corners. Doug thanked God his Mustang had new tires. The tread was great. Stan on the other hand drove an older Jeep and hadn't taken care of it.

"Doug, you're scaring me," Honey whined.

"Honey!" he yelled, holding a hand up in her direction, threatening to slap her if she kept on.

She was right, of course. Driving at this speed was foolish, especially with the weather the way it was, but slowing down meant death.

They needed to get to the next exit if they hoped to reach any place with enough people to make the thing think twice about attacking them. It would take a lot of people, he supposed. A gas station wouldn't do it. A police station would be best, but even someplace as packed as a bar or a bowling alley might work.

This was one of those things people would have to see to believe, and even then, they probably wouldn't believe their eyes.

"Please, baby," Honey begged. "I'm scared too, but you're driving too fast and, in this rain, we might—"

"Just shut up!" he barked.

He didn't have to look at her to know she'd be hurt. Any time he raised his voice at her, she either broke down in tears or came close to it. There was so much more to worry about tonight than her feelings. Comforting her had become a drag lately. Right now, it wasn't important. *Survival* was.

Honey fidgeted with the stereo. He considered stopping her. This wasn't the time to listen to tunes, but then again, maybe it would help calm their nerves. He hadn't seen *the thing* since it had attacked Meg, but he knew it was out there and was coming.

Static filled the radio, surely caused by the storm.

The windshield wipers did their best to sweep the water away, but it was coming down so hard it sounded like the glass was being riddled with bullet holes. Honey changed channels, searching through the stations for music, but the rain came down with such ferocity it overpowered the radio.

Then he heard it. Singing.

An old man singing a song that instantly made Doug's shoulders tense. It reminded him of a tune they sang in Sunday school when he was a kid, but if this was a religious hymn, it wasn't from a Christian church. The lyrics called forth the fire and fury of Hell but in such a way that Doug could imagine the singers dancing happily around a stage as if they summoned a mighty god willing to give them all the warmth and wealth of a life truly deserving.

The old man sang, "Bring yourself up until they all burn down," and behind him, like a background singer, an old woman's voice backed him up at the chorus. "For the fire will lick 'em and will tear 'em all down."

Honey changed the station.

"Wait, go back," Doug demanded.

She didn't have to. On the next station, a pop song started but was interrupted by the old man and the old woman singing. Their voices thundered over the pop anthem until it toned down and disappeared altogether. Now, it was only the older couple belting out that sacrilegious tune. "For the beast will greet 'em and will tear 'em all down."

A face flashed before his eyes like it was coming at the windshield in 3D.

An old man Stan had bumped shoulders with at the last rest stop they'd visited before reaching the campsite.

Doug and his brother were headed into the bathroom when it happened. Stan had walked in while the old man was walking out. Being a big dude, Stan almost knocked the guy over.

"Oh, shit. I'm sorry, sir," Stan had said.

The old man glared at him with big, bushy black eyebrows streaked with white. He was funny looking. Kind of like Groucho Marx but his brows were wilder, wiry.

"Maybe if you paid attention to what's in front of you, you'd have open eyes," the old man replied.

"What?" Stan asked.

"If you'd listen when spoken to, you wouldn't be such a disgrace," came a voice from behind them.

Doug and Stan turned to see an old woman with grey, stringy hair pulled up into a disheveled bun. It looked like it might collapse and pull her scalp off in the process.

As the two men stared, the old woman raised an old Polaroid camera and snapped a picture of Stan.

"What the fuck?" he asked, trying to cover his eyes from the flash and reacting too late.

She turned the camera on Doug and snapped another.

"What's going on?" Honey and Meg both asked from behind her.

They'd been headed into the women's bathroom on the opposite side of the small building when they'd heard the commotion and stopped to see if the boys needed assistance in dealing with the old hag.

The old woman didn't hesitate. She spun on her heels and took a picture of each of the girls.

"I beg your fucking pardon," Meg said. "You can't just go around taking pictures of people without their permission."

"I only ask permission from Father Hezekiah and *his* lord who sits upon the dark throne," the old lady replied.

"The fuck?" Honey asked.

"I think they're high," Meg said with a chuckle. "Look at them." She pointed at the old lady and then at the old man. "They're high as fuck."

"Disrespectful—" the old lady started but was interrupted by her husband.

"They will learn," the old man said. "They'll learn when the wrath is set upon them."

A wicked smile spread over the old lady's face. She pointed at Meg and said, "Yesssss." Her long, bony finger circled a spot in the air in front of the young harlot's face. "Firsssssst."

"First?" Meg repeated.

The old woman laughed and then held her arm out to the side as if expecting her husband to grab hold and begin square dancing with her. He glared at Stan and Doug with his brow furrowed. Meg was right. His eyes were red, crusty, and he looked high as a kite.

"You have yourselves a good evening," Doug said, wanting to end the interaction with the two so he could take a piss.

The old man slinked his arm through the woman's and then walked out, careful to hold the door for her. On their way out the old man mumbled, "Let the wrath be set upon them."

"That was fucking weird," Stan said.

"You had to bump into that old bastard, didn't you?" Doug asked.

Stan laughed. "He's lucky I didn't crush his puny ass against the wall."

Now, speeding down the highway, Doug couldn't get the old couple out of his mind.

The singing continued, and he was sure it was them.

He glanced into the rearview mirror. "Where's Stan?"

"Huh?" Honey asked.

"My brother," he said. "I don't see his lights."

"Well, how could you, driving at this fucking speed?" Honey replied. "I told you to slow down."

Doug, against his better judgment, slowed and pulled over to the side of the road.

"What are you doing?" Honey asked.

"I just fucking told you. My brother needs to catch up with us."

"A second ago, all you wanted to do was drive at—"

"Honey, if you don't shut the fuck up, I'm going to slap the shit out of you."

Her jaw dropped. "Did you just fucking threaten me? I have never—"

Ignoring her, Doug threw the car into drive, slammed his foot down on the gas, and sped over to the grass median that was now a pool of mud separating the lanes. He swung the Mustang around and headed in the opposite direction.

The highway felt incredibly void of life. He'd only seen a couple of eighteen-wheelers since leaving the campsite. It was late at night and most people didn't set out for long drives along West Virginia's interstates in this kind of weather.

Stan had warned him that it was supposed to storm this weekend, but they couldn't let bad weather ruin their trip. Their tents could handle a little rain. Now, Doug wished like hell they'd waited for clearer skies or had picked a faraway location. He couldn't help thinking a slight change in plans could have altered everything. They might still be off somewhere partying and enjoying themselves. Meg would still be alive.

Doug didn't have to drive far before he saw headlights in the opposite lane. He slowed the Mustang as he approached and saw his brother's Jeep pulled over alongside the highway. The driver's side door was ripped off the hinges and lay in the middle of the road.

"What the fuck?" Doug mumbled.

A guardrail blocked the median, making it so Doug couldn't drive around like he had before. Fear washed over him, and he considered whipping the car around and speeding back the way they came, which would have meant driving the wrong way on this side of the highway.

But this was his brother. He couldn't leave him. What if he was alive and needed his help?

Doug pulled the car over and parked on the side of the highway.

"What are you doing?" Honey asked.

"Stay here for a second," Doug told her. "I have to see."

"Doug, no. You are not leaving me here."

"Then come with me."

"Are you crazy?"

"Stan's my brother."

"I know he's your fucking brother, but you saw what that thing did to Meg. If you go out there, you're dead."

"Maybe not. Maybe it left."

He opened his door and the wind brought rain into the car. It slammed against his face.

"Doug, please," Honey begged, grabbing hold of his arm and trying to keep him in the car.

He shook free from her grasp. "Either come with me or stay here and wait."

She let go and shook her head.

"Keep the doors locked until I get back," he told her.

She closed her eyes, and he stepped out of the car and into the pouring rain.

Lightning flashed across the sky, casting a purplish glow over the highway. Doug couldn't help thinking the scene looked haunted. He glanced back at his car and could barely see Honey looking helplessly back at him through the tinted glass. He'd parked on the far side, the safest side, near the tree line. Keeping her out of harm's way wouldn't be any good if she ended up getting torn apart by an eighteen-wheeler barreling down the highway.

Another bolt of lightning slashed the sky and thunder cracked a few seconds after. When the night darkened again, Doug scurried over the metal guardrail separating the lanes, hopping away before any lightning could fry him.

He came upon the Jeep door first. Doug held a hand up to shield his face from the torrential rain as he squatted down to get a clearer look at it. Its hinges were warped, the metal ripped free, where the beast had torn the door off.

Light shone from his right and a horn blared.

Doug leapt out of the way and rolled across the ground as an eighteen-wheeler truck sped past in the next lane over. It barely clipped the side of the door and caused it to spin across the highway as the monstrous truck hauled ass right past him, flinging wind and water his way.

He'd been so awestruck by the mangled door that he hadn't even considered the fact that he was squatting down in the middle of a dark highway frequented by long-haul truckers.

"Holy shit," he said.

His back was up against the Jeep's rear tire. Now wasn't the time to relax.

"Doug!"

It was Honey. She'd left the comfort of the Mustang for him. Perhaps she did love him. He pulled himself to his feet and stared at her across the highway where she stood in the pouring rain, worried about him and calling out to him.

He waved a hand at her. "I'm okay!"

"Thank God!" she replied.

"Get back inside! You're getting soaked!"

"What?!" she yelled.

"Doug," he heard his name whispered from a few feet away.

He turned and looked toward the interior of the Jeep through the gaping hole where the driver's side door used to be. Blood covered the upholstery, had splattered across the inside of the windshield, and was dripping from the dome light.

"Stan!" Doug yelled, running toward the front of the Jeep to get a closer look.

"Dougie," Stan said, calling him by the name he'd given him when Stan was six and Doug was four.

Doug crouched to get a closer look inside to see his brother had scooted to the passenger seat and now sat with his back to the passenger door. Stan clutched the gaping wound across his belly with both hands, doing his best to hold his guts inside. Intestines slipped through his fingers and threatened to unravel in his lap.

"It's bad, huh?" Stan asked.

"It's . . . " Doug struggled to find the right words. "It's not good."

"I'm gonna die here."

"Doug?!" Honey called.

"It's not . . . " Stan tried. "It's not . . . it's not safe for her out there."

"I know," Doug said. "Hold on."

Doug turned to look at Honey and saw the darkness creeping out of the tree line behind her. It seemed to move under the cover of night, slinking through the inky blackness.

"Honey!" Doug yelled. "Get in the car!"

"No!" she replied. "Not without you!"

"Get in the car!" he tried again. "It's behind you!"

It took her a second to understand, then she did, and her face twisted in fear. She lunged for the Mustang door, but the thing, whatever it was, moved much faster than she could.

The darkness enveloped her.

Honey screamed.

Her head came off her body with one swift movement. It smacked against the Mustang window and hit the ground.

The rest of her body seemed to take a few seconds longer to fall. When it finally did, it crashed backward against the car before hitting the asphalt. Blood spurted from Honey's neck, seeping onto the highway and blending with the rain, running downhill with the natural slope of the road.

Doug stared, dumbfounded.

He knew then that he was in love with Honey. His soul practically evacuated his body when he saw her fall.

"Doug, run!" Stan called out from behind him.

But he didn't move.

Not even when the darkness turned toward him and shot across the highway, barreling straight at him. Not even when its teeth tore into his throat and rid him of his pitiful existence.

Only Stan was left clinging to life, shivering, and pissing himself. He bled to death listening to the sound of the beast chewing through his brother's flesh.

Next to him, the stereo turned on, and an old couple sang, "For the beast will greet 'em and will tear 'em all down."

CHAPTER 2

"**C**AN YOU BELIEVE somewhere in all this wild and wonderful West Virginia wilderness is where the next Moonshine Madness rally will be?" Ansley asked from the back seat of the SUV.

Of all Melanie's friends, Ansley was the wildest. They'd been close since kindergarten and had every intention of rooming together at West Virginia University, something Melanie's boyfriend, Tucker, wasn't fond of at all. Ansley had been obsessing over attending the next Moonshine Madness rally, an annual get-together put on by all the area's bikers and moonshiners at a secret location to be revealed only to those who were "in the know." It was meant to be a peaceful event among warring outlaw organizations to help gather money and donations for a children's hospital.

Ansley claimed to know a guy named Motown, from a motorcycle club called Kin of the Fallen, who was going to get her the details this year. She hadn't stopped talking about it since.

"We might be the only chicks at WVU able to attend the rally," Ansley bragged.

"Sounds like a blast," Melanie said, only to appease her friend.

"As long as I'm invited, too," Tucker added.

"Yeah," Ansley replied. "I don't think so." She laughed. "Can you imagine Tucker at a biker rally?"

"Can you imagine *me* at a biker rally?" Melanie asked. She knew she was far from the bad girl type. Ansley's laugh said she knew it too. "Besides, we haven't even discussed it yet, but are you saying WVU is a definite yes for you?"

Ansley shrugged. "Honestly? I don't know where else I'd go. Both of my parents graduated from there, my sister will next year . . . "

Sean had weaseled his way onto their campus tour trip with a lie about possibly attending the school. He only did it to mask his real intentions of trying to get Ansley in the sack during their planned camping trip on the way home. He put his arm around her as he asked, "You really think it's a good idea for a hot young blonde like you to be traipsing around an outlaw festival like that?"

Ansley raised a corner of her lip in disgust as she lifted the stud's muscular arm and let it plop off her shoulder. "A hot young blonde like me?" She rolled her eyes. "Me and every girl in Morgantown, right?"

Melanie couldn't help but laugh. If the idiot had only known her friend had actually been into him on the ride out to the college town. Of course, she'd played hard to get the whole ride out but some of her flirting had been obvious. He hadn't realized it, because the moment they reached Morgantown, he'd been gawking at every girl that walked by and Ansley noticed. She wasn't the type to play second fiddle to anyone. Sean had blown his chance without realizing he'd had one.

"None of those girls at WVU have anything on you," Sean replied.

Melanie glanced in the rearview mirror and, even though Ansley was staring out the window, refusing to look at the boy, she was pretty sure she saw her friend blush.

Yep, there it is. Dimples. Ansley is smiling, but she'll never let Sean see it.

"You really pulled out the big guns on that one, bro," Tucker said to Sean from the driver's seat.

"Easy for you to say, asshole," Sean shot back. "You have a girlfriend."

"She's pretty great, isn't she?" Tucker replied, glancing over at Melanie, and giving her a wink.

Melanie felt butterflies in her stomach. She was so in love with her boyfriend. They'd started dating their junior year of high school and were still going strong. He was a proud member of the basketball team. She was the morning anchorperson on the school news crew.

As she watched Tucker, she admired his quirkiness, like how he always drove with both hands on the wheel at nine and three as if practicing for his upcoming driver's test. He was that kind of guy. He took everything seriously, which was one of the reasons Melanie loved him.

ROAD WRATH

She knew Ansley thought they were a boring couple. While the *hot blonde* had nine sexual partners since losing her virginity her freshman year, Melanie was still a virgin. While Ansley was out partying every chance she could get and was at the lake with friends every warm day, Melanie and Tucker never missed Taco Tuesdays with his family or Spaghetti Thursdays with hers. They went to whatever school event was happening Friday night together to show school spirit, spent Saturdays having movie nights alone, and went to church every Sunday.

Life wasn't perfect, but it was pretty great, and she never rubbed it in anyone's face.

"Love you," Melanie said.

"Love you too, baby," Tucker replied.

"Eww, you're even making me sick," Rowena called out from the seat farthest in the back.

Rowena was once best friends with Melanie and Ansley until she stole Ansley's ex-boyfriend. She'd broken the girl code, and things had been rocky ever since. Melanie and Row (as her friends called her) got along well but Row and Ansley only tolerated one another. She was supposed to have gone on this trip with her boyfriend, but he flaked on her, and she'd asked Melanie to tag along.

"Goal number one – accomplished!" Melanie shouted with a fist pump to the air. "Annoy all my friends with love for my man."

"You do know that's going to fall apart when you get to college, right?" Rowena asked.

Ouch. That was unnecessary.

One of the things Melanie had started to loathe about her friend was her negativity. Ansley's wild side had balanced things out, but since the three rarely hung out together anymore, dealing with Rowena's cynicism was dampening to the soul.

"Maybe not!" Tucker came to Melanie's rescue. "Maybe it'll only amplify. Like, what if when we get to college, our love shines so bright it burns the whole institution to the ground?"

"Could happen," Melanie agreed.

"Totally could," Ansley said, only to tick Rowena off.

"Or," Rowena argued, "what if you're busy doing guy stuff? Like, what if you're in a frat and you're doing whatever frat guys do? You're measuring your cock on a pool table next to eight other cocks and then having sorority sisters suck 'em. I don't know. Just guessing that's what frats and sororities do. And then, while you're busy flinging your dick around, Melanie is out partying with Ansley, 'cause we all know how our girl likes to party. And suddenly they're in a three-way with some big Greek dude named Alfredo until his cousin Giacomo comes in and then it's a full-on orgy and Melanie's calling out his name and—"

"That's enough," Ansley snapped.

Sean was cracking up.

Tucker was silent.

Melanie was at a loss for words.

"Or maybe your love will burn the whole campus to the ground," Rowena said. "You're probably right."

"Fuckin' bitch," Ansley mumbled.

"What did you call me?" Rowena asked, sitting rigid in her seat.

"I think you fuckin' heard me," Ansley replied.

"Ladies," Sean said. "Come on."

"Nah, let her repeat herself," Rowena said.

"I called you a dumb bitch," Ansley replied as she leapt toward Rowena.

Sean caught her and held her back. Rowena jumped forward. Sean tried holding Ansley with one arm while pushing Rowena back with the other. Only the seat between the girls assisted until Melanie climbed from the front passenger seat to the second row to get between the girls.

For a second, Melanie considered pulling out her phone and filming the situation, as it looked like Sean was a lion tamer stuck between two ferocious felines. Fingernails slashed every which way, and he spit hair from his mouth as pieces of Ansley's blonde mane and Rowena's black stuck to his tongue as he cried out for them to stop.

Melanie hesitated at first but decided she better step in when Sean caught an elbow to his jaw, winced, and swatted wildly with open hands of his own as he tried to catch the wrists of both girls' slapping palms.

"That's enough!" Melanie yelled.

"She can't talk to you like that," Ansley said. "She doesn't get to do that. You don't deserve that."

"I can talk to whoever I want, however I—" Rowena started.

"And that's why you're a bitch!" Ansley interrupted her.

Both girls swung a final hand at each other, both missed, and both connected with Sean's face.

ROAD WRATH

"Fuck!" he yelled. "Right now, you're both bitches!"
Tucker was the first to laugh, chuckling from the driver's seat. Rowena followed. Ansley started right after and then Melanie was laughing, too. It took Sean longer to find the humor in the situation.
When the laughter died down, Melanie asked, "Row, what's wrong with you?"
Rowena looked at Melanie and couldn't keep eye contact with her. She lowered her gaze.
"What's wrong with me?" Rowena asked into her lap as shame set in. "What's wrong with her?"
"No, I mean what's wrong? What's going on?" Melanie asked. "You've been quiet most of the trip. You've been in that backseat. You've pretty much kept to yourself the whole time. It's not like you."
"She's crazy, that's what—" Ansley started in.
"Ans," Melanie said, "please."
Ansley stopped.
"Row," Melanie said.
"Cohen dumped me," Rowena said.
"Aww shit," Melanie said.
"Really?" Ansley asked. "That piece of shit dumped you?"
Rowena nodded. "Yeah. That's why he didn't take me to WVU. And why I asked to come with you guys."
"Oh, Row, I'm sorry," Melanie said.
"I'm pretty sure he's fuckin' somebody else," Rowena said. "I found some texts on his phone. And some pictures. He's definitely fuckin' somebody else. I tried to pretend it wasn't what it was. 'Cause, like you said, I'm a dumb bitch."
"I didn't mean that," Ansley said.
"But it's true," Rowena replied.
"No, it's not," Melanie assured her.
"I told you not to trust that asshole," Ansley said.
"I know," Rowena said into her lap.
"Uh . . . rest stop coming up," Tucker called. "I'm thinking it's a good time to stop. It's the last one before we get to the campsite."
"Yes, please stop," Melanie said.
"Your wish is my command," Tucker replied.
"Yeah," Rowena agreed, fanning her face with her hand. "I need to do something about my makeup, and I'm pretty sure I'm missing the lashes on my left eye."

III

Everyone laughed except Sean.

"Your lashes?" he asked. "Thanks to you I'm almost missing the *eyeball* from my left eye!"

CHAPTER 3

TUCKER WAITED FOR everyone to exit the SUV before pressing the button a couple times on the key fob until the vehicle honked, letting him know the doors had locked. Ansley and Sean ditched everyone else and made their way to a row of picnic tables to the right of the small visitor center and lit cigarettes.

Melanie shook her head as she watched her friend blow smoke and fan it away with her hand. She always found it interesting when she did that. It was a strange custom to inhale lungs full of smoke only to fan it away like it was bothersome once it exited her mouth.

"I thought she quit," Rowena said, sucking from a small black plastic device in her hand and blowing a cloud of smoke away.

"Row," Melanie complained, mimicking Ansley by fanning away the girl's vape trail.

"My bad," Rowena said. "I'll blow it the other way."

"She did quit," Melanie replied.

"So, she might actually like this douche then."

"Seems that way."

"Sean's not all that bad," Tucker said as he grabbed Melanie's hand. "He just likes to play the cocky ladies' man."

"Ansley's type," Rowena said.

"Ain't that the truth," Melanie agreed.

"Well, I'm not gonna stand here and watch them all day," Rowena announced. "I gotta pee."

She turned and made her way toward the visitor center. It was a small, grey brick building with double glass doors at the front.

"Me too," Melanie said as she let go of Tucker's hand and followed. She looked over her shoulder when she realized her boyfriend wasn't tagging along. "You coming?"

"Yeah, in a second. I was getting kind of tired driving. I want to see if the vending machines have an energy drink or something to wake me up. At least a candy bar."

Melanie followed Tucker's gaze and saw that the vending machines were in a separate building from the bathrooms. The snack shack looked like the main visitor center but was smaller and was located at the other end of the sidewalk, maybe fifty yards away.

"Want anything?" he added.

"Chocolate," she said.

"Just . . . chocolate? Like, anything chocolate?"

"Like, anything chocolate. I'm easy that way."

"Anything chocolate coming right up."

She watched him walk away and thought about how lucky she was to have him in her life. She reached for the cross pendant she wore around her neck, the one he'd bought her a few weeks ago for her birthday and pulled it out from beneath her shirt. She rubbed at it with her thumb and said a silent prayer.

Looking over at Ansley, she thought about all the sadness her friend carried deep inside. They'd had so many discussions about depression. Things had happened to her at a young age, sadly, at the hands of a youth pastor. Because of that, she'd shunned all things having to do with religion. She pretended to have this hardened, tough exterior when Melanie knew the truth. She was hurting inside.

It was that pain that often kept her reaching out to the wrong kinds of guys. Her need to be loved and cherished in the short term left her with long-term battle wounds and scars.

Sean said something that made Ansley laugh.

Yep, she'll sleep with him tonight. It'll only take a couple of drinks and she'll be the one pursuing him.

Melanie shook her head and walked into the visitor center.

She used the bathroom, and when she went to the sink to wash her hands, she found Rowena fixing her makeup and adjusting her lashes.

"Bitch can't fight, but she can fuck up some lashes, let me tell you."

"You gonna be okay, Row?" Melanie asked.

Like Ansley, Rowena had a tough exterior. Only where Ansley had suffered sexual abuse as a pre-teen, Rowena came from a lower-income, inner city area. She had an alcoholic mother that physically and mentally abused her most of her life. She'd been in a few abusive relationships, too. She'd fought back a couple of times, and one could argue she'd done most of the abusing. As Rowena reminded Melanie the day she explained all this to her, hurt people hurt people.

"I'll be fine, sis," Rowena said. "I can't lie and say it doesn't hurt. It does. Real bad. The thought of him puttin' it to some other chick . . . it hurts. And she's Latina, too. He went from dark brown to a lighter shade of brown. Her name is fuckin' Angelica. Do you know how that sounds in Spanish? They say their Gs like Hs." She said the girl's name again, only this time pronounced it so it sounded like *"Anhelica"*, but when she did it, she sensually shook her hips. Melanie couldn't help but laugh.

"I'm sorry," Melanie said as she continued to laugh. She repeated. *"Anhelica."*

"He's probably fucking *Anhelica* right now," Rowena said. They both laughed.

"You deserve so much better," Melanie said.

"I don't suppose we're gonna find anybody on this trip before we head to the campsite. So, I'm gonna be the odd man out. The fifth wheel."

"It'll be fun. Don't worry. You won't even notice."

"Please," Rowena said. "You and Tucker will be all over each other. Now, Ansley and Sean. And then there's me."

"Ex . . . ex . . . excuse me, an . . . anybody in there?" came a deep, stuttering voice.

The face of a tall, heavyset man wearing coveralls and a dirty light grey sweatshirt popped his head in. He wore a Pittsburgh Steelers hat and thick Coke bottle glasses.

"We're in here," Melanie replied, "but we're done."

"I just na . . . need to clean's all," the man added.

"Yeah, we're headed out," Rowena said.

The man gave her a once over and smiled. It didn't seem like he was trying to be a pervert, but unfortunately, he was coming across as one. Melanie glanced at his nametag as they exited the restroom and saw it read: Mitch.

"You could invite Mitch," she teased her friend quietly.

"Fuck off," Rowena replied.

"I'm just saying. He seemed to think you have the goods."

"Mel."

"Fifth wheel it is then."

"Whatever. I'm going out there with Ansley and Sean. Maybe if I play my cards right, I can slide into a threesome with them." Melanie might have thought she was serious if she hadn't caught her friend's wink on the way out the door.

Melanie was about to follow her friend outside when the display rack full of West Virginia travel pamphlets caught her eye. When she was a kid, she'd grab every pamphlet available at every rest stop her parents visited. She'd collected them the way boys her age collected baseball cards.

She'd had Disney World, Universal Studios, and Busch Gardens from Florida and Cedar Point, King's Landing, and the Columbus Zoo in Ohio. She'd kept them all in her dad's old tacklebox, and if one played their cards right, she might've been willing to trade Tennessee's Dollywood for a Pennsylvania's Hersheypark.

As she approached the visitor center's tiny assortment of West Virginia offerings, she felt a small spark of that childlike excitement ignite inside her.

Melanie picked up a pamphlet for the Mothman Museum in Point Pleasant and looked over some photos of people skiing and enjoying some of the other attractions at Snowshoe. She envied the adventurous thrill-seekers trying white water rafting in the Gauley River. She wondered if Tucker would be willing to go with her if she got up the nerve. Melanie was supposed to visit the Trans-Allegheny Lunatic Asylum last Halloween but chickened out. She'd heard stories about that place. She didn't even want to pick up the pamphlet. Right next to it was one about the West Virginia Bigfoot Museum.

"We have a Bigfoot Museum?" she said aloud.

"Wha . . . why, yes, ma'am," came the deep voice of Mitch, right over her shoulder.

He was standing so close he could practically press his chest against her back. She jumped and dropped the pamphlets she was holding.

"I . . . I . . . I didn't mean to scuh . . . scare you none, ma'am."

"That was awfully close, don't you think?" she asked.

"Wha . . . what was?"

"How close you were standing."

He dropped his head down, looking at his feet, ashamed. "I . . . I don't know. I didn't ma . . . mean anything by it."

Melanie was about to bend to pick up the pamphlets she'd dropped when Mitch held out a hand to stop her. His sleeves were pushed up to his elbows and she saw that his arms were covered in a variety of tattoos. For some reason, that comforted her. He seemed more normal than she'd first thought. It took a certain amount of character to pick out the designs he had on his skin, and it took patience to sit in a chair long enough to let someone do that kind of work.

You know who else shows character and has loads of patience? Serial killers. Don't be naïve, Melanie.

"Na . . . no," he told her. "I've . . . I've got it."

He squatted, scooped up the papers, stood, and handed them to her.

"Thank you," she said.

"I ra . . . really didn't mean to scare you. I wa . . . work here. I'm Mitch."

"It's okay, Mitch. I'm Melanie. Nice to meet you. I should get going. My friends are waiting for me."

There was something in his eyes she couldn't quite understand. At first, she'd thought it was creepy. Now, she thought it might be more like a childlike amusement and she felt bad for judging him. He waved goodbye and she turned to leave.

Outside, she saw Rowena sitting at one of the picnic tables. Ansley and Sean were headed toward the visitor center. When she glanced toward the small building off to the side where the vending machines were located, she didn't see Tucker.

He's sure taking a long time getting a drink and some chocolate. Unless he went to the bathroom when I was in the bathroom.

That was possible. She'd spent time in there talking to Rowena. She figured it wouldn't hurt walking to the vending machines to see if he was still over there. She couldn't imagine why it would take this long but remembered he'd been waiting on a call from their guidance counselor about one of his missing grades. If his counselor called, Tucker might have stayed over there to talk privately.

As Melanie walked along the sidewalk to the snack building, she heard a rattling engine. Glancing over her shoulder, she saw a rust-colored pickup truck pulling a small, old-fashioned aluminum camper as it drove into the parking lot for larger vehicles and trucks towing trailers, which was over by the snack building.

When the truck drew closer, Melanie heard music blaring from inside the camper. It sounded like discordant worship music from church, but old, like it had been recorded in the fifties or sixties. People clapped along to the music. It was part of the track, like it was recorded live. Other than that, Melanie couldn't understand the lyrics, but the people singing along were definitely into it.

Melanie felt herself wanting to clap along to the music or stomp her feet as she walked, but then her ears caught hold of one line in the lyrics that seemed to suddenly clear up among the muffled sounds floating on the wind. It was like she was meant to hear that part of the hymn. "The beast is coming to snatch your soul."

Her fists clenched as something moved through her. It was anger—no, anger wasn't the correct word—it was more like disgust for the sound, but the feeling came on so automatically that it seemed to act like a protective barrier seeping through her skin from within, forming a wall around her. The music could no longer reach her, but she knew it was out there. It was trying to get to her, to expose her to its haunting melody and unbalanced symphony.

The sight itself wouldn't have seemed strange to her. This was West Virginia. Many of the state's residents were elderly and drove vehicles that had been in their family longer than they had. A lot of them were good, churchgoing, God-fearing folks. But the people playing the music coming out of that vehicle worshiped a different god. A dark one.

One she imagined might have slipped into the mind of a serpent long ago and slithered over to an innocent Eve, convincing her to try the forbidden fruit.

Melanie turned away from the truck and kept walking toward the snack building, hoping Tucker would step out of the door and meet her on the sidewalk. She would feel a lot better with him by her side. He would probably laugh and dance a little jig to the music. His ability to make light of most situations always seemed to calm her nerves. Now was one of those times. She felt eyes on her back and knew someone was watching her.

She glanced over her shoulder. There was a man and a woman seated in the truck, with the man in the driver's seat. The sun's reflection across the windshield made it impossible to see what they looked like, but Melanie was sure the man wore a hat. His hair was scraggly and stuck out of the sides of his cap. Next to him, the old woman wore her hair in a bun. They were watching her.

Melanie turned around and kept walking. It occurred to her the smart thing to do might be to hightail it back to her friends, but that would mean passing the truck, and she wasn't ready to do that. Moving forward felt like the right thing to do.

Out of sight, out of mind. Just get behind that closed door.

There was the sound of a record scratching and then the music inside the camper suddenly halted. Then there was dead silence.

She looked over her shoulder again and saw that the old couple inside the truck were still watching. They didn't move. They could have been wax figures.

Melanie turned away, picked up her pace, and entered the snack building. As the door closed behind her, she thought she heard the truck's door opening. What mattered was she'd made it into the building. She threw her back against the door and rested there, gasping for breath as if she'd sprinted the whole way.

She closed her eyes and inhaled through her nose, exhaling out her mouth. A laugh escaped her as she thought of how silly she was acting. It was nothing more than some old locals. She'd probably misunderstood their music.

Yeah, that's all it is. You misunderstood the lyrics.

Melanie rolled her eyes and laughed again, embarrassed at her childish behavior.

Inside, the building was empty and dim. The bulb was out in the one overhead fixture. The blue fluorescents from the vending machines provided the only light and filled the room with an eerie electric hum.

There were six machines in total. Chips, cookies, candy, and chocolate bars filled the three on the left. The three on the right held a variety of drinks. One was a coffee and espresso machine and the other two contained a mixture of water, juice, energy drinks, and soda.

What absolutely wasn't in the room was Melanie's boyfriend.

Now, she was faced with turning around and walking back outside to face the two creepy old people with the staring problem.

"Dammit, Tucker," she whispered.

It wasn't his fault. Thinking back, she should have offered to come with him to pick up snacks. Then they could have gone to the bathroom at the same time. But she'd wanted to check on her friend. That had been the real reason she'd gone to the bathroom first.

Melanie reached for the door handle, yanked it open, and shrieked.

CHAPTER 4

MELANIE COULDN'T STOP the scream that erupted from her throat. She hadn't expected to open the door and find the frail old man standing in the doorway, staring at her with bushy black, grey-streaked eyebrows and snow-white hair that curled in thin wisps from his black cap. His mustache matched his hair but had brown streaks under his nostrils and Melanie swore there was snot caked there.

His eyes were bloodshot. When he smiled, his teeth were rotten. Most were chipped and grooved in different places. To Melanie, it looked like they were made of wood and had been set on fire only to be put out quickly, leaving behind random burn marks.

They reminded her of the grooves in her grandfather's ashtray. When she was a kid, back when he was still alive, she'd often curl up on his yellow banana couch—that was what she called it because of its bright yellow color—and watch TV while stealing glances at the tendrils of grey smoke that ribboned toward the ceiling from the cigarette he always had perched in that plastic ash catcher.

The ashtray had stains like this creepy old man's teeth from the many cancer sticks that had burned to the filter and scorched it.

Melanie shifted her gaze downward and her eyes fell on the brown vest he wore over a white dress shirt that was stained yellow. Tan slacks several sizes too big for him, covered his bottom half. His shoes were on their last mile. The big toe on his right foot looked like it might pop out soon, like a groundhog testing for spring.

He reminded Melanie of Geppetto from *Pinocchio* if the wooden boy's father was scarier than hell. This old man looked like he wanted to pick the meat from his teeth with her teeth—or anyone else's for that matter. His grin was the most sinister thing she'd ever seen and the wiry hairs protruding from his nostrils threatened to reach out and grab hold of her wrists at any moment. If the hair from within his ears didn't get her first.

You're being judgmental. He's somebody's grandfather. Somebody's father. Somebody's husband. He's just old. Probably sweet. Old and sweet.

"Slow down, girl," the old man said.

"I'm sorry, sir," Melanie replied. "I didn't know you were coming in."

"Well, where the hell else would I be going ta?"

At first, she was taken aback by his rudeness, but she remembered her grandfather and how bitter he'd become in the later stages of his life. He snapped at everyone most of the time but years earlier he'd been one of the nicest men she'd ever known. Dementia was a monster.

She didn't know this old man's story, and as much as he freaked her out, the fact remained that he was a senior citizen and might have been through some tough times in his life that had left him upset with the youth of today.

You're better off dishing out a little respect than rancor. The world needs more Mary Poppins *and less* Rawhead Rex.

Melanie was a fan of musicals and horror movies, and often thought you could distribute the world evenly into one of those two boxes. Everyone seemed to either have their heads in the clouds and not understand what was going on, as if believing the world was one big dance number, or they were always angry, bitter, and horrific. She kind of wished people could just be honest with themselves about the state of the world and choose to be nice to each other.

Now was her opportunity to put her money where her mouth was.

Melanie bit her tongue as she said, "Right."

She stepped aside and held the door for him.

He didn't enter right away. Instead, he looked at her like he was surprised by her reaction. Perhaps he'd expected a bad attitude from her and wasn't sure how to react when she didn't give him the sass he'd anticipated. It was either that or he couldn't understand her manners. Maybe he'd never seen a woman hold a door for a man before.

Cautiously, he stepped into the room with a shake of his head. His face lit up in electric blue from the vending machine lights reflecting off his pale face.

His mouth hung open and his tongue lolled out. Melanie expected drool to drip from it onto the floor, but none came. If she didn't know better, she would have thought he was seeing soda and candy for the first time.

Melanie's eyes were on him when she let go of the door. It was heavier than expected and slammed shut. She jumped and let out an audible gasp. The old man noticed and turned to gawk at her. He grinned and made a clicking sound with his tongue. Her shoulders tensed and her back went rigid.

"Squirrely one, ain'tcha?" the old man asked. "Or you's just scared of an old man?"

Hearing him say it out loud made her feel foolish. There wasn't a whole lot the old man could do to her. He was so thin, so frail.

He clicked his tongue again and the sound made her think of giant cockroaches crawling over one another. She shook the thought from her mind, unwilling to let the old man spook her.

"It wasn't you," she said. "The loud bang caught me off guard is all."

He nodded and grinned again. Then he turned to look at one of the machines. He shoved his hands into his pockets and stared slack-jawed at the offerings.

Every bone in Melanie's body told her to get out of the building. To run back to her friends, get in the SUV, and get as far away from the old man as possible.

Then there was a different part of her that thought he seemed sad. Like he'd stepped out of a time machine from back when people traded glass Coke bottles in at the gas station, and he didn't quite understand what he was now seeing in front of him.

Tucker was a fan of everything 80s and 90s. They'd recently watched the entire *Back to the Future* trilogy, and the old man reminded her of Marty McFly visiting the futuristic diner in *Back to the Future 2,* when he didn't understand how to open the Pepsi.

Melanie took a deep breath and decided to do what she felt was right and offer him assistance.

"Did you need help with something?" she asked. "Was there something you were looking for?"

The old man looked at her and raised one eyebrow. He still seemed unsure about her. Then he turned his attention back to the candy bars.

"Snickers," he said barely above a whisper and laughed. "LifeSavers? I think not. PayDay. Ain't that the truth."

Maybe it's money then? Maybe he doesn't understand these new machines only take credit or debit cards?

Her good nature got the best of her, and she couldn't stop herself from asking, "Do you need some help making a purchase from the machine?"

The old man turned to look at her and squinted his eyes. He took a step closer.

Melanie felt a change in the environment around her. The air became heavy and damp. She felt beads of moisture on her arms and each inhale was warm and sticky, like she was breathing with a mask on.

The sensation reminded her of the time she'd chosen to wear a scary rubber mask for Halloween and regretted it all night because of the difficulty she'd had breathing with it on.

It was like someone had thrown sand in her eyes. She found it harder to open her eyes with each blink. She was so sleepy.

The old man's thick, bushy eyebrows twitched as he gave her body a once over. "Help? You think you can help me?" He laughed. "Oh, girlie. You're the one who needs help."

He raised a fist as if he might bring it down on her like a hammer—like he had every intention of striking her.

Melanie threw her hands up, ready to defend herself and push the man away, but the motion seemed slower than her normal reaction speed should have been. The old man suddenly stopped with his fist raised in the air and focused on her chest.

"Hmm," he said. "What is that?"

He reached out to touch her, but she moved away.

"Keep your hands off me," she replied, fighting the urge to call him a creep.

She'd lost the ability to remain in control of her emotions. Fear was now running the show.

As she stepped toward the door, she followed his gaze and saw that he was looking at the small cross pendant she wore around her neck. It had been like a shield against his attack. The moment he saw it, his fist hadn't been able to come an inch closer.

Melanie fought through her sleepy haze and moved away from him. "Look, I don't know what your problem is, but I'm gonna go now. My friends will be worried about me."

The old man took a step back and laughed. "Friends. Ha! Know what the Book of Hezekiah says about friends?"

She pushed open the door and started on her way out. She'd never read the Bible from front to back, but she'd been fed pieces of all the books within it by different preachers and pastors over the years. She didn't remember there being a Book of Hezekiah. This caused her to pause in the doorway and think for a second.

Was there a Book of Hezekiah?

"It says friends are the enemies you've not yet made," the old man informed her. "For only your brothers and sisters in darkness will press naked flesh against yours and dance in the blood spilled from the blade of the dark lord."

That, Melanie knew for certain, was not in her Bible. This old man needed help, and it was the kind she couldn't give him. Her moment of hesitation was over, and she launched herself through the cracked-open door, so she didn't have to hear another word of his maniacal rambling.

The second she reached fresh air the world sped up again. Her limbs were free of the invisible chains of lethargy that had been keeping them weighed down. The sluggishness was gone. It was like she'd been kicking for the lake's surface and the old man's dark aura had been clinging to her ankles and holding her down.

Melanie gasped for breath and ran right into Tucker's chest.

"Whoa, Speed Demon," he said.

She hugged him tightly. "Poor choice of words."

He laughed and let his arms fall around her, pulling her body tight to his. "What's this for?"

"Let's go. There's a really creepy old man in there saying some freaky stuff and—"

Tucker instantly went into defensive boyfriend mode, interrupting her explanation. "Did he say something to you? Wait, did he *do* something to you?"

"Yes," she started to explain then changed her mind. "No! Tucker, please. Let's get the others and get out of here."

Tucker pulled free from her. "If that guy did something then—"

"Tucker, please! I want to go."

Her boyfriend's posture relaxed, and he grabbed her hand, his eyes still glued on the snack building.

"Come on," she said, turning him away from the doors and

pulling him down the sidewalk. As she led him by his hand, she saw the old couple's truck. The cab was empty.

Where is the old lady?

She didn't know why the woman's absence bothered her so much. This was a rest stop. People stopped here for a reason—to use the *rest*room.

Melanie picked up her pace. She felt the need to reach her friends and usher them back to the SUV before it was too late.

Too late for what?

She didn't know. It was simply a feeling she had.

"Mel," Tucker said. "What's the rush?"

"No rush," she replied.

"No?" he asked with a chuckle. "Could have fooled me. And the arm you're about to rip out of its socket."

"I'm sorry. I just want to go."

They were halfway down the sidewalk that led to her friends when she saw the old lady walk out of the visitor center. Now that she wasn't seated behind a windshield marred by a reflection, Melanie got a clearer look at the woman. She wore old brown boots and an ash-colored dress that matched her dry, straw-like hair pulled up into a bun. Over her dress, she wore a brown leather vest. It had big pockets in the front that bulged with whatever items she kept stuffed inside.

It was the woman's face that drew Melanie's attention. Her eyebrows were drawn on in thin black pencil, in nearly perfect triangles. If the narrow, squinty shape of her eyes and blackness of her eyeballs didn't look so cold and mean, those eyebrows would have given her that appearance on their own. Her face seemed unnaturally smooth for her age, and her thin lips gave her unsmiling mouth a stoic grimness that was difficult to look at.

With Melanie's focus on the woman's face, she almost didn't notice her hands. Her fingertips, except her thumbs and a couple of others, had bandages on them. Chipped, cracked nails poked out of their frayed ends.

The woman's entire appearance was unsettling.

If there was ever a perfect match in this world, this old woman, and the old man she'd arrived with, were it. Melanie could only assume they were husband and wife. The big brown rock on the old lady's left ring finger said she was married.

That ring finger was now curling into a balled-up fist as the old lady stopped walking toward her truck and stood with her knuckles on her hips only a few feet from where Melanie's friends sat at picnic tables smoking and gossiping. With their backs to the visitor center, they didn't see the old woman standing so close to them.

"Hurry," Melanie said to her boyfriend.

"What? Why?" Tucker asked.

She let go of his hand. He wasn't comprehending the severity of this situation. She caught up to the rest of the group in time to see Rowena blow out a cloud of vape smoke. Ansley and Sean, who were back outside smoking again, took their final drags on their cigarettes and flicked the butts somewhere in the grass.

"Smoking, huh?" the old lady asked.

Rowena gasped and coughed out more smoke. She'd been caught off guard by the woman's sudden appearance.

Ansley and Sean both laughed. Neither responded.

"I'm sorry," Rowena said. "I didn't even know you were there."

"The devil's left hand will smack you," the old lady said, "while his right will pat your back. Then both will come together and stroke your ego until you collapse into orgasmic bliss. And don't we all love orgasmic bliss?"

"What the fuck?" Ansley asked.

"Old lady kinda has a point," Sean said.

Behind them, the visitor center door opened, and out stepped Mitch, the big man in the coveralls and the Steelers cap. "Is . . . is . . . is everything all . . . all right out here, fa . . . folks?" he asked.

The old lady turned and waved him off like he was an annoying gnat. "Go inside, Mitch. Ain't no business of yours. Not unless you want it to be."

"Na . . . no, Mrs. Vilma. No, ma'am." Mitch waved and Melanie thought he was waving at her. Then he went back inside the visitor center.

Mitch knows the old couple. They're not travelers. They're locals.

The old lady turned back to the young adults and cracked a smile that showed yellow teeth through her thin-lipped grin. "Got an extra cigarette?" she asked.

Ansley looked at Sean, who shook his head.

"Afraid not," he said.

Melanie had heard the entire conversation and had now reached the group. She stopped. Tucker caught up to her and stood behind her.

"I think we should get going," Melanie informed her friends. "Now. Let's get back to the Chevy."

"Do you have a cigarette?" the old woman asked Melanie.

Melanie shook her head. "I'm sorry. I don't smoke."

"Hmm," the old woman said. "Hot smoke. Scorch the lungs. Good. Like burned flesh as we will all blister and peel when we go to be with the dark lord."

"What the fuck is your problem?" Sean asked.

"Just go get in the car," Melanie said.

"You do not worship?" the old woman asked Sean.

Sean seemed to find the whole ordeal entertaining. He laughed and said, "The only thing I worship is . . ." His eyes fell on Ansley's ass, and she squealed in fake embarrassment. Melanie knew her friend loved the attention.

The old woman didn't find his comment comical. She glared at Sean. "I was wrong about you," she said. "I thought maybe you were believers."

"Believers they are not!" thundered the voice of the old woman's husband, causing Melanie and Tucker to jump.

The old man was moving toward them down the sidewalk.

"Believers of what?" Tucker whispered.

"Something evil," Melanie informed him. "Let's go."

Still, nobody moved. They were all too busy being entertained by the quirky couple.

"No?" the old woman asked. "I suppose you are right. Believers they are not."

"These two are seriously warped," Sean mumbled.

"I think Melanie's right," Rowena said. "We should leave. They're only trying to antagonize us."

"I'm sorry," Ansley said. "Antagonize us? I don't even know what the fuck is going on here."

"Well," the old lady said, "if you're not harlots for hell, then I suppose you must be heathens for heaven. Jezebels for Jes—"

Melanie didn't let her finish. She'd had enough.

"Listen, you old wench," Melanie said. "You can follow whatever deity you want, worship your own demons, and bow down to whatever false idol you desire, but you've crossed a line speaking blasphemy on my God—"

"Turn the other cheek, missy," the old lady whispered, her tone quiet and raspy.

"Go fuck yourself," Ansley said.

"How dare you—" the old man started.

"Meh," Sean interrupted, "you go fuck yourself, too, you Satanic prick."

The old lady giggled but the sound seemed to come from within her chest. It grew louder until it was a full-on laugh. Before long, it increased to a loud cackle and her husband joined in. Now, both were laughing. The sun was weakening in the sky as Melanie and her group stood outside the visitor center watching these two old folks laughing hysterically. It wasn't only strange, it was demented. She almost expected them to suddenly stop and tell her this had all been a prank orchestrated by Ansley.

The old lady pulled an old Polaroid camera out of her large vest pocket and snapped a picture of Ansley and Sean.

"What the hell was that?" Ansley asked.

"Did she just take a picture of you?" Tucker asked.

"The old bitch took a picture of us!" Sean said.

The old woman pulled the photo out of the front of the camera and shook it in the evening air before shoving it into her pocket.

"No, no, no," Rowena said. "You need to give us that picture. You can't take pictures of—"

The camera clicked, the flash went off, and Rowena's eyes went wide before she squinted and fought through the blindness. The old lady pulled the photo from the front of the camera and shook it, right in front of Rowena's face.

"You were saying?" the old lady replied.

"You bitch!" Rowena yelled.

"Now, now!" the old lady said. "There will be none of that."

Tucker reached for the camera, but the old lady turned and snapped a picture of him. She had the camera ready and fired off another picture of Melanie.

The flash blinded Melanie and Tucker so neither saw the old man's hand come up holding a strange weapon that consisted of a leather handle fixed to a two-foot piece of razor wire.

It happened much faster than anyone would believe the old man capable of moving. He slapped the piece of wire around Tucker's wrist, let it wrap around him, and then yanked back, sawing its metal teeth into Tucker's flesh. Those ferocious pieces of sharp razor bit into the upper portion of the young man's forearm and into the soft skin at the bottom of his wrist, ripping him open.

Melanie noticed a blur of movement out of the corner of her eye and glanced down in time to see blood spurt from her boyfriend's arm and splash onto her shoe.

Tucker didn't scream.

His lips curled back over his teeth like a sound might erupt from his throat loud enough to tear the night in two, but the only sound that came out was a garbled, confused, long-winded sigh that seemed to carry on it a painful cry for help.

At first, only Melanie seemed to notice his wound.

Rowena was the next to see the blood. She covered her mouth and shouted, "Oh my God!"

Then Ansley saw it. She'd never done well with blood, so her immediate reaction was to lean forward and vomit. Melanie didn't look but heard wet chunks hit the sidewalk and smelled the remains of Ansley's partially digested meal.

Sean ran to Tucker's aid and got there as the old man pulled his razor wire weapon away and gestured for his wife to follow him back to the truck.

"Melanie, lift his arm!" Sean yelled. "Fuck! Put pressure . . . um . . . I mean. Fuck. Tie something around his wound."

"Tie what?" Melanie asked.

Her mind was racing a hundred miles per second. She couldn't calm down and think clearly. Tucker was shocked.

"That's so much blood," Tucker said. "I'm gonna fucking die."

"You're not gonna die, man," Sean said, pulling his shirt off and tying it around Tucker's wrist. He lightly slapped Melanie's shoulder and said, "Keep his arm elevated."

Sean, now wearing only the white tank top he'd had under his shirt, turned toward Rowena and said, "You, call the cops."

Melanie held Tucker's arm up and watched as Sean stalked after the old couple walking to their pickup truck.

"Hey!" Sean yelled. "Where do you think you're going? You're gonna stay here 'til we get the cops out here, you freaky fucks."

Rowena tried emergency services and looked back at Melanie. "It's not working."

Ansley tried her phone. "Same."

Rowena walked toward the visitor center. "That guy, Mitch. He can call for us. There has to be a phone in there." She reached the door and yanked on it. It didn't budge. She pulled on the one next to it and it too was locked. They all were. She looked back at Melanie. "The doors are locked."

"What?" Melanie asked. "We were just in there."

Rowena slapped on one of the glass doors with an open hand. The lights inside turned off.

"Mitch!" Rowena yelled. "Open the door! Please! We need your help out here! Please, I know you're in there! Open the door!"

She turned back to Melanie and shook her head. Melanie glanced over at Sean and saw him push the old man, who then turned around and swung the piece of razor wire at him. Sean easily dodged it.

"Are you fucking kidding me?" Sean asked.

"Sean!" Melanie yelled. "Leave them alone. Let them go! Get their license plate and let them go!"

Sean backed up a few steps. "I should beat the shit out of both of you right here in this parking lot," he threatened.

"Yes, stay," the old woman said.

"Sean, come on!" Melanie called out to him. "The phones aren't working, and that guy locked us out of the visitor center. We have to get Tucker to a hospital!"

Sean used his phone to take a picture of the old couple, he took one of their truck and the plate in front and then ran around to the back to get one of the license plate on the camper it pulled.

"Go ahead and leave," the old woman said. "Wrath will be set upon you."

The old man cackled and repeated, "Wrath will be set upon you!"

"Fuck you and all your wrath," Sean yelled as he ran back to his friends.

CHAPTER 5

"**W**HERE ARE HIS keys?" Sean barked from behind the steering wheel.

Ansley slid into the passenger seat while Melanie and Rowena helped Tucker into the second row, wedging him between them. Melanie leaned Tucker's arm against her shoulder.

"Keep your arm there, baby," she whispered. "Keep it there so it stays elevated."

Tucker shivered. His lips trembled.

"I can't drive without his keys," Sean said. When nobody answered, he clapped his hands loudly and shouted, "Mel! Where are his fucking keys?"

"I . . . I don't know," Melanie said before leaning closer to her boyfriend's ear and whispering, "Tucker, baby, your keys?"

Tucker tried to fish them out of his pocket but was having a difficult time, so she pushed his hand away, retrieved the keys, and tossed them to Sean.

"Don't worry, buddy," Sean said. "We're gonna get you to a hospital."

"Where?" Rowena asked. "There isn't one around here."

"We have to go back," Ansley said.

"Back?" Rowena replied. "Back where?"

"Back to Morgantown," Ansley said. "Back to Ruby Memorial."

"Dude, WVU's like thirty, forty-five minutes away," Sean argued. "He's already turning pale."

"Just go!" Melanie shouted. "Go to Ruby. It's the only hospital, Sean! Just drive already!"

"Okay, okay!"

Outside the SUV, Melanie swore she heard choir music, and the sound soured her gut. Her stomach ached like she'd eaten something bad, like someone had forced her to feed on a dozen rotten eggs. Instant nausea overwhelmed her as she imagined the old couple celebrating in their truck while she and her friends anguished over what to do about Tucker's wound.

"Do you hear that?" Melanie asked.

Rowena cocked her head to the side. "Hear what?"

"That music."

Rowena was quiet and then said, "Sounds like church music, right? I hear it but faintly."

As Sean sped out of the visitor center parking lot, the music faded, and with it, the nausea she felt.

Storm clouds seemed to follow them as they left the visitor center and the moment the SUV touched the highway, the sky let loose with torrential rain. It pounded the vehicle's roof and pelted the windshield so hard it was nearly impossible for Sean to see where he was going.

Sean drove at a high speed anyway.

"Slow down!" Ansley squealed. "You're gonna throw us off the side of the mountain!"

"I can't slow down," Sean argued. "We need to get him help."

"It's not going to matter if we all die trying to get him there," Rowena pointed out.

"I don't care," Melanie said. "Drive as fast as you can without killing us."

"Yes, ma'am," Sean said.

"That's fucking helpful," Ansley said and put a hand to her temples to massage her head.

"These wipers suck ass," Sean complained. "I can't see shit."

"Where did this rain come from?" Ansley asked. "It was clear earlier."

"It . . . it was supposed to be clear all night," Tucker said, his teeth chattering in the process. "I . . . I . . . checked the weather."

"Shh, it's okay," Melanie assured him. "Don't worry about it. We've all been in the rain before. We'll be in it again."

"But the camping trip," Tucker said.

"I don't think we're gonna be camping," Rowena said under her breath.

Melanie slapped her arm.

"What?" her friend said, defensively.

Melanie raised an eyebrow in her direction. Rowena nodded, understanding now wasn't the time to be negative. Tucker needed to believe everything would be fine and they'd continue their trip as planned as soon as they'd taken care of his arm.

"Those fucking freaks," Ansley said.

"I should have beat the shit out of that old man," Sean said.

"You should have!" Rowena agreed.

"There wasn't time," Melanie argued. "We had to go. Besides, what good would it have done? We'll get to the hospital and call the cops. That old couple can't be hard to track down. Not with the pictures Sean got. And that guy Mitch at the visitor center knew them. We can tell the cops that."

"It's better you didn't attack the old bastard," Ansley agreed. "You'd be looking at an assault charge when this is all over."

Thunder clapped overhead.

Sean tapped his fingers against the steering wheel as he leaned forward and tried to see through the water swooshing back and forth across the windshield. His voice came out shaky as he spoke. "It still feels wrong letting them go like that."

The words barely made it out of his mouth when something slammed into the left side of the SUV. Sean hit the brakes and the vehicle's tires screeched, fighting for traction on the slick highway.

"What the fuck was that?!" Rowena yelled.

"I think something – someone hit us," Sean said.

The next hit came from further back at the rear of the SUV and nearly caused them to spin.

"What the fuck, man?!" Sean shouted. "Someone's trying to run us off the road!"

Melanie looked out the side window and saw the pickup truck from the visitor center. The old lady was in the passenger seat, and she waved at them while smiling. Her sinister grin forced chills down Melanie's spine.

"It's the old couple!" Melanie announced.

"They followed us?" Ansley asked.

Sean slowed down.

"What are you doing?" Ansley asked him. "Don't slow down. Speed up!"

"I want to let them pass us so I can—"

He didn't get to finish his statement before the truck careened into the front end of the SUV. Sean tried to hold the wheel steady, but the road was too wet, the vehicle hydroplaned, and they went spinning out of control. Unluckily for them, they'd been hit on the left side and skidded to the right, where the side of a mountain awaited.

With no guardrail to stop them, the front end of the SUV whipped around, fell into the roadside ditch, and jerked to a stop. The rest of the vehicle didn't, and the occupants inside braced themselves as they flipped upside down.

The roof of the SUV smashed against the rocky terrain. Melanie, who'd been wearing her seatbelt, jerked toward the floor which was now also the ceiling but was slammed back when the airbags deployed. Searing pain cut into her collarbone as the fabric of the belt bit her skin.

"Ugh!" she cried out.

Things crunched around her, and glass crackled. The windshield had to be falling apart but she couldn't focus on it at the moment.

Rowena lay under her, or above her, as it were. She hadn't been wearing her seatbelt and now she was lying across the broken sunroof. Her forehead was bloody, and she wasn't moving.

"Row," Melanie said. "Row, are you okay?"

Rowena moaned but didn't answer her.

Tucker, who'd been belted in at the waist in the middle seat, still dangled upside down. Melanie struggled with the airbag in front of her, pushing and shoving it away from her so she could see his face. His eyes were closed. Blood ran from his wound and dripped on Rowena's thigh.

"Tucker," Melanie said. "Tuck . . . Tucker."

"Mel," Tucker squeaked out.

"Oh, thank God," she said.

She could hear Sean and Ansley whispering in the front seats. Sean unfastened his seatbelt and fell. He helped Ansley out of her seat. They both crawled out the passenger side window as the driver's side was blocked by solid rock. Sean appeared a moment later, lying down, with his head in the broken window frame of the back seat.

"Is everyone okay?" he asked.

"Does everything look okay?" Rowena mumbled.

When she lifted her head, she was missing a couple of teeth and a river of crimson saliva ran down her lip and chin.

Melanie prepared herself for the pain that was about to come and then pushed the button on her seat belt. Her body collapsed and she covered her head to protect herself from impact as her knees collided with the airbag. It didn't hurt nearly as bad as she thought it would. Rowena cried out as Melanie landed on her ankle, hurting her more than she'd hurt herself.

"Sorry, Row," she said.

Rowena pulled herself to a leaned-over upright position and rubbed at her ankle. "Bitch."

She forced a smile back at Melanie to let her know she didn't mean it.

"Want to help me free Tucker?" Melanie asked.

Rowena looked over at Sean.

"I don't think I'll be able to get in there," he said. "This thing's pretty crushed. We'll be lucky to get you guys out. If you can unlatch him and help him fall, I should be able to drag him out."

Outside the SUV, Ansley stood watch and kept an eye up on the road. "Umm, guys, what do we do if the old couple comes back?"

"I don't think they're coming back," Sean said. "They got what they wanted. And they'll want to get as far away from this as possible. Hurting Tucker was one thing, but they could try to claim self-defense. You know, say we tried to attack 'em or something. But this . . . they clearly ran us off the road. Their truck has to be fucked up, too."

"Okay, you ready?" Melanie asked.

Rowena nodded. She'd squatted down on the other side of Tucker and was holding onto him the same as Melanie. Melanie unlatched the seatbelt and Tucker's heavy body fell.

"Shit!" Melanie yelled, doing her best to stop him from crashing to the ground.

"Oh, fuck," Tucker cried out.

"Got you," Rowena said.

Neither of the girls had him. Not really. He crumpled to the ground hard and lay there whimpering. He'd grown even paler, and Melanie feared he wasn't going to make it much longer. The shirt Sean had tied around his arm was now soaked completely red.

"All right, Rowena, come on out," Sean said.

She carefully crawled out of the SUV.

"Why don't you two go up to the road and see if you can flag down any passing cars," Sean suggested.

"And what if the old couple—" Ansley asked.

"I told you—" Sean said, getting frustrated.

"We got it," Rowena said. "We'll look for someone who can help."

Sean nodded. "Thank you. Anyone. A truck driver, anybody really." He pulled his cell phone out of his pocket. "I still don't have a signal on my phone. See if yours works. We need somebody to get us out of here and get Tucker to the hospital."

"Okay," Rowena said.

Rowena and Ansley marched up the steep incline from the SUV to the highway.

Inside the SUV, Melanie stroked Tucker's hair.

"He's having a hard time staying awake," she told Sean when his face appeared in the window.

"Don't let him fall asleep."

"I know."

"I'm gonna grab him under his armpits and try to pull him out. I might need you to push from your end."

"Push where?"

"I don't know. Wherever you can really."

Sean slid into the SUV on his belly and reached under Tucker's arms. He wrapped his hands under Tucker's armpits and gripped him tightly.

"When I count to three, I'm going to pull. Maybe put your hands under his thighs and do your best to lift and push."

Melanie grimaced. "Okay."

Sean got to his knees for leverage. "One . . . two . . . "

Melanie moved between Tucker's legs and reached under his thighs, preparing to push him.

As Sean was about to call out the third number, his voice wavered. Something wasn't right. A look of concern came over him.

Melanie watched as the young man's handsome, confident face changed. His brow furrowed and then his eyes shot open. Someone, no, *something* was behind him.

Two hands reached over Sean's shoulders. Fingers spread out, long black digits with jagged fingernails. When the fingers closed over the young man's shoulders, they made a click-clack sound as they settled into place, like bones breaking.

The hands appeared to be human, only larger than any Melanie had ever encountered, and the skin was charred black. Brittle pieces of skin were flaking off to expose a reddish color underneath, like charcoal bricks dying out as they faded to full ash.

"Sean?" Melanie squeaked out, afraid that if she spoke any louder it might startle the owner of those hands.

Sean's eyes glanced left. He was trying to get a glimpse of whatever was behind him grabbing.

It was too late.

With one sudden jerk, his body was yanked out of the window, pulling Tucker out with him.

Both men were snatched clear out of the vehicle.

Sean let out a terrified scream.

Melanie crawled out. She acted purely on adrenaline, following her boyfriend's body.

The rain had stopped. Tucker and Sean were nowhere in sight.

"Noooooooo!" Sean screamed and the sound echoed all around Melanie.

Her eyes darted left, then higher as the treetops shook behind the SUV above where they'd crashed—where rock ended, and the trees began. Whatever had wrenched him free of the vehicle had scaled the rockface and was now carrying him deep into the forest. Sean's screams ricocheted off the mountain, and boomeranged around trees, assaulting Melanie from every direction.

She tried to figure out where his voice was coming from, but one second it was above her while the next it came from around the curve ahead. Then she could have sworn the boy cried out from the other side of the highway.

He was everywhere all at once.

"Sean!" Melanie yelled. "Tucker!"

It couldn't have carried away Sean and Tucker—

"Mel!"

Tucker's voice sounded weak, but it was close.

"Tucker?" she tried again.

"Here," he said.

She walked along the creek bed and didn't have to go far before she found her boyfriend lying in the water where the thing had dropped him. The right side of his face was bloody, mashed against a large stone that acted as a pillow and kept his mouth and nose above water.

He lay on his stomach with most of his body in the water, including his cut arm, and his legs were splayed out at an awkward angle. Not broken, just one leg lying over the other in a strange, scissored position.

"Tucker!" she yelled and rushed to his aid.

She gingerly pulled him away from the water and cradled him in her lap. "My God. Were you dropped like this?"

"I think so," he said.

Sean's screams rang through the air once more and turned into agonizing shrieks. It sounded as though he were being ripped apart, piece by piece.

Tucker lifted his face off her lap and his expression twisted into one of terror. "Is that Sean?"

She could have lied to him, but what would be the point of that? If they were going to get out of this alive, they needed to be on the same page. Everyone did. "Yes," she said.

"Melanie?" Ansley called out.

"Over here!" Melanie yelled.

"Over where?" Rowena replied. "Where did y'all go?"

Rowena and Ansley stumbled down the rocky slope and stopped near the creek, close to the SUV. Melanie waved a hand to get their attention.

Sean was quiet now and Melanie knew he was dead. The thing that had grabbed him by the shoulders had torn him apart.

And probably ate him.

She wasn't sure why that last part came to her, but she had the feeling it was a beast of some sort. It would eat meat. Even the human kind. She knew she shouldn't have accepted Sean's fate so easily, but she also didn't have a choice in the matter, and whining about it wouldn't get her anywhere.

Somehow, she and her friends had stepped out of that musical part of life she sorted things into and into the horror side. The rules had changed. They needed to learn them quickly if they had any hope for survival, and they needed to get far away from here.

If she'd had more time to process what had happened to Sean, Melanie might have broken down.

It was a good thing she didn't.

Ansley and Rowena cautiously went to where Melanie sat with Tucker, stroking his hair.

"Girl, what are you doing way over here?" Ansley asked.

Both girls seemed to notice the blood on the side of Tucker's face, and both looked into the stream and the bloody rock that had recently acted as Tucker's pillow. Rowena looked back at the SUV.

"Did you hear all that screaming a second ago?" Rowena asked.

Melanie didn't have an opportunity to answer before Ansley looked back at the SUV and then over at Melanie and her boyfriend quizzically. "Mel, where's Sean?"

CHAPTER 6

ANSLEY STOOD NEAR the SUV staring up at the rockface. Unlike Melanie, she wasn't taking this well. Instead, she seemed to be in shock.

When Melanie first explained what had happened, Ansley refused to believe it. Shaking her head, she said, "People don't fly away, Mel. They don't just fly away." Then she repeated it as she walked back and forth through the creek, uncaring whether she soaked her shoes. She stared up as if expecting whatever had taken Sean to bring him back.

Rowena was quiet, like she wasn't quite sure what to make of it. At least she was helping Melanie with Tucker while Ansley seemed to be in her own little world.

"We need to go," Melanie said. "It was real, Row, and it's going to come back for us."

"Maybe it was a monkey," Tucker said with a lazy grin.

He seemed to have forgotten that he'd been whisked away by the beast himself. He'd probably gotten a clear look at it, but his mind seemed fractured. Half the shit he said didn't make sense.

"It wasn't a monkey," Melanie said.

They'd been over this already. Melanie had done her best to clean the wound on his arm and wrapped it with a piece of a flannel shirt she found in the back of the SUV. The sun was setting, and the sky was a pretty piece of pastel, like saltwater taffy was stretched over the trees that ran along the other side of the highway.

We always got the best saltwater taffy at Myrtle Beach. What I wouldn't give to be at Myrtle Beach right now instead of on this messed-up stretch of highway.

"Maybe it was *Tarzan*," Tucker said.

If the situation were different, Melanie might have found her boyfriend's behavior comical. If he'd had a few too many tequila shots or if she'd been burdened with the task of driving him home after a root canal and the anesthesia was doing a number on him. This wasn't one of those moments and comedy wasn't convenient.

"Yeah, he needs help," Rowena said. She turned to look at Ansley. The pretty blonde was disheveled and distraught, still looking up at the mountain top. "Ansley, honey," Rowena called. "We need to get going. It isn't safe out here, and the sun's gonna be gone in a few minutes."

Ansley shrugged her arms out and hands up to the sky, still so full of hope. "We have to wait for Sean. I know he'll be back."

"Ans—" Rowena challenged, but Ansley was having none of it.

"You'll see! Any minute now he'll come down this mountain and—"

Something struck Ansley in the head. She stopped talking and rubbed her head. "Oww."

She looked down, bent over, and picked up the thing that had fallen on her. She held it up so Rowena and Melanie could both see.

Melanie couldn't believe her eyes. It looked like a human rib bone picked clean.

Another fell from the sky and hit Ansley on the shoulder.

"Ouch," the girl complained and covered her head with her arms. "What the fuck?"

A third rib bone missed Ansley and landed on the ground next to her. Then a fourth. Small bones came falling after, riddling the ground.

Melanie rushed to her friend who stood frozen in place. She grabbed Ansley's arm and pulled her away. As they raced away from where she'd been standing, Melanie looked down and saw that the small bones pelting her friend's skin were human teeth. Other bones hammered the earth all around them.

"They're bones!" Melanie yelled at Rowena. "Help me get Tucker up! We have to get out of here now! That thing's above us!"

Rowena helped Melanie lead her boyfriend through the creek. Melanie stopped and looked back at the SUV.

"Hold on," she said, leaving Ansley with the others, as she raced back to the SUV.

"What are you doing?" Rowena asked.

The back of the vehicle had burst open when it landed upside down. Melanie leaned in and moved stuff around until she found what she was looking for. She pulled out a tire iron. She crossed the creek and met her friends on the other side.

"Weapon?" Rowena asked.

"Yeah, if it has to be," Melanie said. "We might also need it to break the window at the visitor center."

"The visitor center?" Ansley asked.

"We can't go back there," Rowena said. "We need to get Tucker to the hospital and Morgantown is the opposite direction."

Melanie started up the steep incline that led toward the highway and was already walking at an angle that led away from Morgantown. "We can't walk all the way to the hospital. It's impossible. We're closer to the visitor center. There has to be a phone in the office."

Rowena shook her head. "You mean the office of that guy who locked us out of the building the last time we were there?"

"Mitch. Yes."

"What makes you think he's going to let us in?"

"It's the only option we have. If he doesn't . . . " Melanie held up the tire iron.

"But if Sean comes back—" Ansley started.

"He's not coming back!" Melanie and Rowena shouted in unison.

Whose ribs do you think those were? Whose teeth?

As much as she wanted to say the words aloud, she couldn't bring herself to be that mean. Ansley may not have realized they were pieces of Sean's skeleton bouncing off her skull and shoulders a minute ago and perhaps it was better that she didn't.

"I'll stay here and wait," Ansley insisted.

Melanie wheeled around and faced her friend, grabbing Ansley by her left shoulder with her free hand. "I know it's difficult to understand, but you didn't see what I did. That *thing* is still out there. It took Sean and he's not coming back. If we don't get out of here quickly, it's going to come back for us."

"But why?" she asked. "Why is it coming for us?"

"I don't . . . " Melanie started to say she didn't know but as she was thinking of an explanation, her eyes drifted over Tucker's arm. "The old couple," she said.

"What?" Ansley asked.

The wreck had been the creepy old couple's fault, but Melanie hadn't thought the thing that attacked Sean had anything to do with them. As absurd as it seemed, she was sure of it now. They'd wanted to force them off the road so they could sic this *thing* on them.

"It's the old couple," Melanie said a little louder. "They did all of this. They forced us off the road and sent that creature, or whatever it is, after us."

"That's crazy," Rowena said. "It was probably a bear. They're all over the place out here."

"Are they?" Melanie asked.

For a second, the shadow of a doubt seeped in.

Could it have been a bear? No, it had charcoal arms and hands like a human but with long, bony fingers.

Melanie shook her head. "No, it wasn't a bear."

"Fine," Rowena said. "Not a bear. Doesn't matter, really. I hate to say it, but let's hope whatever it was is full now from," she lowered her voice, "eating Sean." Then at full volume, she finished with, "And let's get the fuck out of here. Bring your metal tire thingy and let's go."

Rowena led the group as they walked along the shoulder of the highway. She had nobody to slow her down and she was clearly on a mission to make it back to the visitor center in record time. About ten feet behind her walked Melanie with her arm around Tucker's waist. It wasn't a lover's embrace, and it wasn't to help keep him upright. It was to lead him forward. He kept wanting to stop or wander off to the side of the road.

This left Melanie constantly having to call out to her friend to wait for them. Rowena complained each time but stopped and let them catch up.

Ansley walked about another ten feet behind Melanie and Tucker. She sang softly, more like a humming that Melanie found soothing. Rowena, on the other hand, did not find it calming.

"Can somebody please tell Enya back there to keep it down before she draws that bear monster toward us?"

"Can somebody please tell Oscar the Grouch that I can hear her?" Ansley replied. "And that music calms my nerves?"

"Maybe you should cut out the middleman," Melanie suggested. "Since that middleman is me and you can clearly hear each other fine."

ROAD WRATH

Rowena and Ansley didn't speak directly to each other. Instead, Rowena scoffed and walked faster along the side of the highway. Ansley hummed a little softer.

Melanie had driven this stretch of West Virginia highway many times in the past. This was the main route she'd take to get to Pittsburgh, the largest nearby airport, and she'd never seen this highway so dark and deserted. Only a few cars passed during their long march and all those drivers ignored the waving hands of the young adults trying to flag them down for a ride.

It made her wonder if the old couple had cursed them to walk the earth in total isolation. *Are we invisible to passersby?*

Usually, eighteen-wheelers traversed this highway in droves, hauling cargo from one end of the country to the other. Those drivers were likely to feel bad for a group of young people like Melanie and her friends who were obviously down on their luck and stranded. Yet only a few long haulers had gone by, and none even slowed as they passed.

It was like they were walking inside one of those snow globes people picked up at souvenir shops in foreign countries to keep on their fireplace mantle to prove they'd actually set foot in France, Italy, and Switzerland. Only this globe was a slow walk through hell, and if shaken properly, instead of snow, it might stir up Sean's bones and send them falling from the sky again.

Melanie was aware that her mind was a twisted place. She often had to push intrusive thoughts far from her mind in church. The Devil liked to make an appearance and plant whispered stories in her ears. Those tales sometimes seeped in while listening to the pastor preach. While he explained Paul's strife, she'd sometimes find her eyes wandering over the crowd in the pews until she settled on one person. She'd create an entire fictitious backstory for what brought that person through the church doors.

Once there was a woman named Margaret, which probably wasn't her real name, and she'd been a professor of psychology at a nearby college. Margaret would only give good grades to the students who'd agree to stay after class and attend orgies in her honor.

At that point, Melanie would grab hold of this sinister daydream and force it far from her mind. As soon as she spoke the words, "Lord, please take these intrusive thoughts from my head" they'd disappear, and she'd be more at ease. At peace.

A thought arose as she walked along the highway holding Tucker's waist.

Tucker is slowing you down. What if you leave him here? You can make it back with help before that beast gets to him. And if you don't—

"Lord, please take these intrusive thoughts from my head," Melanie whispered.

"I'm thirsty," Rowena complained.

"Me too," Melanie said.

Her mind was back on the walk. No more negative thoughts. She wanted to get her boyfriend to safety. They only needed to get back to the visitor center. It couldn't be much farther.

Behind her, Ansley continued to hum a tune that sounded like it came from a movie soundtrack, or it could have been a new-age tune. In the beginning, the humming hadn't bothered her at all. Now, it was grating on her nerves.

You could turn around and throw that tire iron at her. If you hit her right in the throat, you could stop that humming permanently.

"Lord, please take these intrusive thoughts from my head," she tried once more.

Her mind settled and she did her best to find peace in her friend's music. She tried to remember it was Ansley's way of keeping calm. She was scared. They all were.

Ansley was in the middle of singing when her voice went from a beautiful hum to a stunned yelp. Then silence.

"Ansley?" Melanie asked, turning quickly to check on her friend.

The girl was there, still standing about ten feet behind her with her arms outstretched. She reached out to Melanie as if waiting for her to run into her embrace so they could wrap each other in a hug. It was too dark to see her clearly, so Melanie took a few steps closer.

"Wait, Mel," Tucker said as Melanie left his side.

"Hold on a second," Melanie replied. "Ans?"

Ansley's mouth opened and closed like she was trying to get a word out, but none would come. As Melanie stepped closer, she saw the look of pain on her friend's face and understood why she couldn't talk. Her throat had been ripped out. She was a bloody mess from collarbones to chin, as if monstrous claws had swiped and torn free a giant chunk of flesh.

"Oh, my God! Ansley!"

"Ansley?" Rowena called from behind Melanie.

Ansley's mouth opened and closed like a fish out of water, trying to catch a breath. Melanie tried to make out her silent words, and they finally became clear: "Help me."

"Ansley!" Melanie screamed as she ran toward her friend.

She was only a few feet away when charred hands with long, chipped fingernails reached around Ansley. This time one grabbed the girl by her bloody throat and the other drove its claws deep into her stomach, puncturing the skin and sloshing all the way in until it had a handful of gut. Unable to talk or scream, a gurgling hiss was Ansley's final cry for help.

Red eyes blinked over her left shoulder. That was all Melanie saw of the thing's face. It was huge but ducked down to stay hidden behind the girl.

With a wicked grunt that said it was finished with the show, the creature wrenched Ansley's body to its right, leapt over the guardrail, and rolled off the cliffside, disappearing into the darkness of the forest.

"No!" Rowena screamed.

Melanie knew screaming wouldn't work.

Tucker was silent. Until he stumbled and fell over.

CHAPTER 7

MELANIE STUMBLED TOWARD her boyfriend, seeing his prone body through glossy eyes. Tears threatened to fall but she wiped them away before they could. Her breath hitched in her chest. Her best friend had just been snatched away by the same dark figure that stole Sean and made his bones rain over the land.

Don't think. Don't think. Keep moving. Get Tucker up and keep moving.

When she reached Tucker, he wouldn't budge. He'd passed out and Melanie knew it was because he'd lost too much blood. She dropped to her knees next to him and tried to shake him awake.

Rowena stood hugging herself with her arms crossed, shaking her head in disbelief as she talked to herself aloud. "Holy shit! Holy shit! Did you see that? It fucking took Ansley. It took her right over the side of the mountain."

Melanie ignored her friend and focused on the task at hand. Freaking out right now wasn't going to help them and Rowena was doing enough panicking for them both.

"Tucker, please," Melanie begged. "I need you to get up, baby. We have to go."

"It took her right over the fucking edge of the mountain," Rowena repeated.

"Tucker, come on."

"It dove right over with her."

She couldn't ignore Rowena any longer. Wiping fresh tears, Melanie looked up at her friend from her kneeling position. "I tried to tell you, Row. I tried to tell you it wasn't a bear. That it was something else."

Rowena nodded vigorously. "I know. You were right. We have to go."

"Try your phone again," Melanie said.

Rowena pulled it from her pocket. "Not even 911."

"They've done something. I know they have."

"Who, the old people?"

Melanie didn't answer her. She had a hard time believing it herself. Instead, she shook Tucker and tried once more to wake him. "Please. You're gonna get us killed. Just wake up and come with us."

He wouldn't open his eyes.

"A car's coming," Rowena said. "I see headlights."

"Flag it down," Melanie told her as she continued to try and rouse her boyfriend.

"It's close!" Rowena warned her.

The car horn blared as it sped past, causing Melanie to jump. Wind whipped at her back and tossed her hair.

"Nobody's going to stop for us," Rowena cried. "I even tried stepping out into the road. It went right around me."

Melanie looked at her friend, then down at Tucker. "Would you stop for us?"

"I'd like to think so." Rowena paused for a second. "We have to leave him."

Melanie shook her head. "We are not leaving him."

"Nobody will stop for us, and we can't move fast enough with him. If we leave him, we can get to a phone and call for help. Then we can send someone to get him."

That was what they always said in horror movies and books. Someone was always left behind with an injury with a promise by the hero that they'd send help. In almost all those stories, the hero returned later to find the friend dead or gone. Tucker wouldn't be here later if they left him, Melanie knew that. That *thing* would take him if they left him.

"I'm not leaving him," Melanie said. "If you want, you can go on without me. You'd get there faster without us behind you anyway. We were slowing you down."

"You were," she agreed.

"It's a good plan then."

"Maybe, but I don't want to leave you, Mel."

"I don't want to leave you, Mel," came a mocking voice from the darkness below. It was whiny and childlike.

"What the fuck was that?" Rowena whispered.

Melanie shrugged. It hadn't sounded altogether human. Only one thing was sure, it was close. Melanie pointed toward the other side of the guardrail. Rowena stepped closer and peered over the side where the mountain dropped off to nothing but darkness and treetops far below.

During storms, Melanie had seen emergency responders, tow trucks, and construction crews lined up alongside the highway trying to haul vehicles up that had lost control and gone over the edge. She'd always wondered what that must be like—those final seconds when someone realizes they can't turn back and they're suddenly flying off a mountainside.

Ansley knows.

"Get away from the edge," Melanie warned.

"Yeah, you're right," Rowena said.

"Get away from the edge," the mocking voice said, again sounding high-pitched and childlike.

"We really need to go," Rowena said.

"Yeah," Melanie agreed. "Tucker, come on."

She'd stepped away from her unconscious boyfriend to peer over the cliff's edge. As she made her way toward him, she saw something dark moving along the side of the highway, pressed against the guardrail maybe fifty feet away. It was moving on all fours, like a dog, but approaching carefully like it was trying to remain unseen. It came from behind, even farther back than where the thing took Ansley.

"Mel," Rowena whispered. "Do you see it?"

"Yeah."

As soon as she confirmed it, the creature dashed forward on all fours, racing toward them. The darkness was its friend, hiding its true appearance in the shadows. It was large, but it didn't have the wide girth of an animal as large as a bear. This thing was much skinnier. Camouflaged in the blackness of night by skin of the same shade, it also had an eerie orange glow that shone through cracks in its skin like hot lava attempting to burst from a hardened shell.

Rowena grabbed Tucker under his arms and pulled, dragging him along the side of the highway, but she was struggling, and they weren't going to make it far.

Melanie looked back at her boyfriend and knew what she had to do. She raised the tire iron and held it like she was taught to wield her softball bat. She knew she didn't stand a chance against this beast, but maybe she could stun it enough to make it think twice about attacking again.

"Are you crazy?" Rowena asked.

"No more than you are, thinking you're gonna outrun it while dragging him!" Melanie yelled.

"You've got a point. I'm sorry, Tuck." Rowena dropped Tucker, turned, and ran.

"Wait, what?" Melanie asked. "Shit. No."

Realizing she was alone, she backed up a few steps until she was closer to Tucker. "Come on, you son of a bitch."

The thing in the darkness snarled and then giggled, sounding like a small child at afternoon recess excited for its sneakers to hit the playground pavement.

It came at her and was now twenty feet, fifteen, ten . . . it could pounce at any second.

As it drew closer, it came into view with the darkness, revealing its features a little at a time. Its entire body was naked, black like it had been dipped in tar with skin that had a charcoal-like roughness and was covered with fine hairs.

Its face was pale, streaked with black ash, like the face of a big . . . baby. Like an infant. No, that wasn't it either. It was almost like a dark, deadly cherub. A childlike cherub's face. She recognized it as something she might see on a Valentine's Day ad, the way one might draw cupid, but this seemed blasphemous, evil, summoned to strike fear and wreak havoc on the world.

The eyes burned fiery red, and its teeth were jagged and razor sharp when it opened its mouth.

But it had no interest in Melanie. Instead of leaping at her as she expected, it waited until it was five feet away, and right when she was about to strike with the tire iron, it swerved left and dipped past.

"Hey!" she shouted. "Leave him alone!"

She swung her weapon and hit air, causing her to spin and nearly fall.

The creature didn't slow one bit.

Rowena was gone, disappeared. Either she'd already sprinted too far ahead, or she'd found a hiding spot.

Tucker lay flat on his back where Rowena had dropped him. He was still unconscious when it happened. For that, Melanie was thankful.

The beast charged him with such speed and ferocity it almost didn't stop in time. When it did halt, it skidded and planted its claws in Tucker's throat to brake. The force of the thing's forward momentum was so strong it ripped the young man's head completely off his body.

In the movies, his flesh might have stretched like gory elastic bands and his spine might have clung to his skull. The scene would have been prolonged. Each disconnecting piece of him would click and snap until it all came apart in a bloody geyser.

But this was real life, and it happened much faster.

Tucker's head flew off and bounced several times along the highway like a stone skipping across a pond. Blood spurted with it, of course, but it all seemed to happen too easily, like his body gave up on him and didn't fight hard enough to keep his head intact.

It didn't seem real, and, for a moment, Melanie didn't believe it was.

Then she screamed, and it all became too real. She dropped to her knees and the tire iron clattered on the asphalt next to her. She continued to wail. Her head felt like it might burst with the pressure from her cries.

She watched through tear-filled eyes, she thought she saw Tucker's fingers twitching.

The creature made a snickering sound that reminded Melanie of a cross between a small child's giggle and a hyena's cackle. The demon-like thing lifted its face to the night and laughed harder before slamming its mouth into the open wound at Tucker's neck and feasting.

Melanie stopped screaming and fought for breath. She felt like she might hyperventilate. Snot dripped from her nose and settled on her upper lip. She wiped it away with the back of her hand and remembered the importance of focusing on what she could do about her situation. Breaking down, curling up in a ball, and cowering in fear would get her nowhere.

Fighting, or continuing to run away, might get her out of this nightmare.

Since they'd left the visitor center, she'd been fighting so hard to stay out of the present and focus only on the next step.

Ok, we've crashed.

Next step? Get out of the vehicle.

ROAD WRATH

Ok, something took Sean.
Next step? Get the others and get to a phone.
Ok, something dove over the side of the cliff with Ansley.
Next step? Wake Tucker up and keep moving.
Ok, Tucker's head is off. It's off. His head is fucking off!
Next step? What's my next step?
What is my next step?
Being rattled wasn't going to help. She needed to reset the panic button if she hoped to get out of this alive.
And how do we face our monsters?
She felt for the cross pendant around her neck and rubbed it as she prayed. "Lord, I can't do this without you. I know I'm not alone out here for you said you would go before me and be with me. That you would never leave me nor forsake me. I believe you. I have faith in you. Be with me now. Help me get through this. In Jesus's name, Amen."

She remembered fearing there was a monster in her closet when she was about eight years old. She couldn't sleep because of it. After lying in bed for about an hour and repeating all the lyrics she could remember from the *Veggie Tales* song 'God is Bigger' she got out of bed with only her bedroom nightlight on, marched right into her closet, and started swinging her fists at every article of clothing while singing that tune. Her parents heard the commotion, her gleefully singing "God is bigger than the Boogeyman" and came in to find her laughing in the closet, covered in clothes. She was never afraid of her closet again.

This situation was a little different, but she knew God was still bigger than this boogie man. She refused to sit here any longer and watch her boyfriend's body be this creature's snack. She took one final mental snapshot to use as fuel for her rage.

"Get off him!" she yelled.

The thing didn't respond.

Slopping, slurping, tearing, and ripping. The sounds of the beast's meal were worse than witnessing the damage.

"I said get off him!" she cried a second time, stomping her feet hard against the pavement and rushing forward.

When she was a few feet away, she threw the tire iron hard and hit the creature on its back. A growl emitted from it, but it barely stopped eating long enough to glance back as blood dripped from its infantile chin. It snickered again and lifted a clawed hand toward the sky before shoving it into Tucker's chest so it could grab hold of his ribcage.

The creature stood upright, gripped the dead young man by its new ribcage handle, and carried him toward the roadside and over the guardrail. Tucker's headless body hung backward in an arch, his arms and legs dangling as the creature carried him like a bodybuilder swinging around a duffel bag.

"No," Melanie whimpered as she watched the monster go.

She was defeated.

The beast was gone. It had disappeared into darkness the way it had twice before.

Melanie looked over at the tire iron lying on the ground and wondered why the beast had allowed her to live. She'd attacked the monster and had been alone. It had killed Sean, Ansley, and Tucker. None of them had done a single thing to it. Yet they were gone. Why did she deserve to live?

Her brief surge of heroism had fled and now she felt like curling into a ball and waiting for the creature to come back and finish her off. She didn't know what else to do. Maybe it would be quick and painless. If the monster didn't come back for her, a car or truck would eventually come along and slam into her, splattering her remains along the highway. Either way, she'd be taken out.

You're being a pussy.

It wasn't a Godly thought. No, this was her older brother whispering in her ear. He was a U.S. Marine and he'd always told her that.

When she'd cried because she hadn't made the softball team the first time, he'd told her, "You're being a pussy. Practice harder and try out next year."

When she'd gotten picked on in the seventh grade and he was in high school, he'd said, "You're being a pussy. This is what you do." Then he proceeded to teach her how to punch her bully in the nose.

Her older brother never took any shit.

He still wasn't taking any shit and now the U.S. government was paying him to not take any shit.

Yes, you're being a pussy. Get up and get out of here so you can send somebody back here to take care of that old couple and whatever the hell this thing is.

After a few minutes of sitting there, she glanced both ways and thought about her dilemma. The reason she'd walked toward the visitor center was to try and get help for Tucker.

Tucker's gone.

His head lay on the highway not far from where she was drooped over. In the darkness, it looked like a lump in the road. It could have been any kind of roadkill. Nobody would stop to check it out. Where it lay, there was a good chance one of the big trucks would run it over and squash it like a melon. Even full-grown deer didn't stand a chance on this highway. Tucker's head would be done for.

It was a morbid thought, and it dawned on her that she should be sadder. How much was enough? She didn't know, but she felt like she owed Tucker more.

The broken heart that would inevitably come with losing her boyfriend would have to wait. She knew that. Right now, she felt numb. Dazed in a way. Her head was fuzzy and crossing over to a strange place that bordered on hysteria.

Yes, a laugh was building inside her.

Not because any of this was funny but because she couldn't believe any of what had transpired this afternoon was real. It was all so absurd.

Glancing once more at her boyfriend's head, she chuckled and was grateful nobody was out here on the road to witness it. They would think she'd gone mad.

"Mel," came a voice from within the shadows a little further down the road.

Is that really a voice or have you actually gone mad?

She decided she was losing her mind. She looked behind her, in the direction of where the SUV had crashed earlier. Should she walk in that direction? Or try to get to the visitor center and the possible phone there?

"Or," she said aloud, "I can walk to Morgantown. It might take me a week but at least I know I'll be going someplace away from those crazy old bastards."

"Melanie," someone called again. "Melanie, who are you talking to?"

She turned around and saw Rowena standing in the darkness. She didn't know what to say. Rowena had run away and left her, but could Melanie blame her? She wouldn't have gotten far pulling Tucker. The beast would have pounced on her and ripped her to shreds.

Melanie laughed and rushed to her friend. "Rowena?"

"What happened?" Rowena asked.

"You ran and—"

"I know. I'm sorry. What happened to—" Rowena's words caught in her throat as she saw Tucker's head on the highway. She cupped her hands over her mouth and sobbed, shaking her head in denial.

Melanie wrapped her arms around her. "You had to run."

"I didn't know what else to do," Rowena said.

"I know."

"But he's dead."

"I know."

"And that thing is going to come back."

"I know."

Melanie only said it because she didn't know what else to say, and as she stood there trying to think of other words, she heard the rumble of an engine approaching from behind them.

"Mel, someone's coming," Rowena said. "Look."

Coming from the direction of Morgantown were a set of high beams.

"We have to make them stop!" Rowena said. "We can't let them pass."

Melanie and Rowena both stepped out into the road and waved their hands wildly. As the lights drew closer, Melanie became worried.

"Wait, what if it's the old couple? What if they were waiting all this time to—"

"It's not them," Rowena said. "There's no way they'd wait that long. They're gone by now. It's been hours."

"Yeah, I'm sure you're right," Melanie said but didn't believe it, as she went back to waving her arms.

It wasn't until the vehicle came into view, and she saw that it was a minivan and not the old pickup pulling a camper, that she relaxed and allowed herself to believe this might be the help they'd been hoping for. With both girls standing in the center of the road, the driver of the van had no choice but to slow down and stop. Through the dark windshield, it appeared there was only the driver in the vehicle.

"Don't move from the front of the van," Rowena yelled at Melanie. "If you don't block him, he might drive off."

"Okay," Melanie said.

Rowena moved around to the driver's side of the van and spoke to him. Then she came back to Melanie and waved her toward the passenger side. "He said he'll give us a ride."

"Oh, thank God," Melanie said as she got into the back seat.

Rowena got in the front passenger side.

The driver didn't start driving when they closed their doors.

"You two look pretty banged up," he said. "My name's Mike. I'm headed toward Mount Nebo. Where you headed to?"

"Anywhere away from here," Rowena said.

"Yeah, but—" Mike started.

"Please, sir," Melanie replied. "Please just drive."

Mike had to be in his mid-fifties. His forehead wrinkled with concern as he winced at Melanie's command. "Sure," he said. "I'll get goin' then. You can let me know on the way."

"Thank you," both girls said in unison.

Mike stepped on the gas and the van moved along the highway toward the visitor center.

Melanie noticed from the backseat that Mike kept looking at Rowena and glancing in the rearview mirror a few times at her. She didn't feel he was checking them out in a sexual way. It was more like he was suspicious.

"How did you two get out here anyway?" he asked as he drove.

"It's a long story," Rowena said.

Melanie was anxious, worried that he wasn't driving fast enough. She looked behind her, out the back window, expecting to see the headlights of the old couple coming up fast, ready to run them off the road like they had Tucker's SUV, but the highway behind them remained dark.

"Look, if you girls are in trouble, I can probably help. I work security at the mall and my brother is a cop over in Webster Country," Mike tried to explain.

"Please, sir," Melanie begged. "Just drive us as far away from here as fast as possible."

"Yeah, sure. Of course."

They hadn't driven far when Mike leaned forward in his seat. He seemed to be focused on something up ahead on the side of the road.

"What the hell is that?" he asked.

"What?" both girls asked.

"Up ahead. Not a deer. A bear maybe."

Melanie leaned between the two front seats to get a clearer look through the windshield. At first, she saw nothing but the blackness of the unlit countryside. Then she caught movement as something large raced along the roadside and scurried up a tree.

"Stop!" Rowena shouted.

Mike slowed to a crawl.

"Turn around," Melanie said.

"What?" Mike asked as he brought the van to about five miles per hour, inching along the highway.

"Turn, please!" Melanie yelled. "You don't understand. It's a creature or something demonic. It killed our friends."

"It what?!" Mike shouted. "I um . . . um . . . I um . . . I need to call . . . " He fumbled with his phone, saw he didn't have reception, and dropped it. "What the fuck, man?"

"Mister," Rowena said, "you have to turn the van around now before it's too late. You can turn here. There's not even a median. Just grass. You can turn around and go in the other direction. Just do it!"

The van crept along, drifting too close to the trees at the highway's edge.

"Right here?" Mike asked. "But I can't—"

Mike hadn't even finished his argument when the thing leapt out of the trees, bound across the highway on all fours, and soared through the air. He froze and watched in horror as it came at them.

All was silent for a moment.

When it crashed down on the windshield in front of Rowena, it landed so hard the glass caved in on her side. The explosion came so suddenly and so loud it caused Melanie to jump and scream.

Mike yanked the steering wheel to the right and the van swerved toward the guardrail.

The creature brought its clawed hand back and ferociously struck the glass, thrashing wildly as it shrieked like a banshee. Its clawed hand beat at the glass, fighting to get to Rowena.

"Get back here!" Melanie yelled as she realized the beast was focused solely on reaching her friend.

Rowena didn't listen. She kept screaming and held her hands up to protect herself.

Mike fought to regain control of the vehicle. "Get off my van!"

The beast turned to glare at him, its red eyes staring with its childish grin.

Mike swerved the van to the left.

"Mel!" Rowena yelled.

It was the last word Melanie would hear from her friend.

The creature turned its attention back to Rowena and with one final attack on the shattered glass, it reached down with both hands, wrenched the transparent shield out of the way, and grabbed hold of Rowena by the shoulders.

"Rowena!" Melanie yelled.

It was still gripping her friend when a loud horn blared. Bright lights shone through the rear of the van, and what felt like a freight train barreled into them from behind.

The world went spinning.

Glass flew in all directions.

Rowena was gone.

Mike yelled.

Mike flopped.

Blood splattered.

More spinning.

A loud crunch.

Thud.

Screech.

Crash.

The punch of airbags deploying.

Weightlessness.

Flying.

Melanie now knew what it felt like to go soaring over the edge of the mountain.

Butterflies in her stomach.

Peace for a moment.

Slam.

Everything hit her.

Was this what death felt like?

Darkness.

CHAPTER 8

EVERYTHING HURT. Melanie's arms, legs, chest, forehead, the corners of her eyes—even the backs of her eyelids hurt. Yet she was alive.

Blackness enveloped the inside of the vehicle, relenting to random shards of blue cast by the moon.

It was enough for Melanie to see that all the van's windows were blown out.

Rowena was gone. So was Mike.

Where the hell am I?

Melanie forced herself to slide to the passenger side door and shove it open. It swung outward way too easily, almost pulling her from the van as it snapped off its hinges and plummeted down the mountain. The door pinged off the rocky cliffside and struck sparks as it tumbled to the bottom.

Holy cow. That was close.

Melanie hadn't realized she was at an angle. The van was leaning toward the front. She raised slightly and peered through the gaping hole in the windshield. The hood was wrapped around a giant tree, keeping the van from sliding the rest of the way down the mountain, like the door had.

The van was also leaning slightly to the right, meaning that tree might not keep her in place much longer. Falling forward wasn't the only way to go. Sliding right would take her down as easily. The thought of moving scared her. Even the slightest adjustment of weight could cause the van to plummet down the mountain.

She closed her eyes and tried not to focus on the pain she felt *everywhere.*

Airbags had deployed in the front but not in the back.

This time it wasn't her brother's words that got her moving.

It was someone else's. She felt for the cross pendant around her neck. Miraculously, it was still there, and she rubbed it as she thought of these important words.

"Truly I tell you. If you have faith as small as a mustard seed, you can say to this mountain, 'Move from here to there,' and it will move. Nothing will be impossible for you."

She didn't need to move the mountain. She only needed to move her terrified ass *off* the mountain. The good Lord might not use her brother's vulgar words when he told her, "You're being a pussy," but that didn't mean His words weren't as tough.

Sometimes simply hearing Jesus ask, "Where is your faith?" is strong enough.

Melanie gritted her teeth and slid her ass to the left until she was at the driver's side door. With no more hesitation, she shoved the door open and stopped it from swinging back at her. Her head fell back, and she almost laughed at her willingness to give up so easily.

Where the right passenger door had led to nothing but open air and freefall down the side of the mountain, the left door opened to solid ground. An entire path of rock and soil led into the forest. There was even a dirt road where people could camp near the cliff's edge.

She was in no immediate danger. The van was on solid ground, or at least it appeared that way. She decided to get out of it in case the right side was as close to the edge as she originally thought. Being confident was one thing, being cocky was another.

Left with no options as to which way she should travel, Melanie walked the dirt road that led into the forest. She had no weapon, and she wasn't a fool. Of her group of friends, she was the last one alive. The creature would come after her now. Unless, of course, it thought she was dead. It must have been a truck that hit the van up there on the highway. Maybe the creature saw the van go over the edge and now assumed she was dead. She doubted that.

As she walked through the dark, quiet forest, she wondered if it might have been smarter to stay near the van. She imagined if the truck driver had stopped, they would have called in the wreck. Cops and other first responders would show up eventually. They'd look for possible survivors and haul the van off the mountainside.

Leaving the accident site was probably the worst idea.

Melanie thought about how no phones worked out here. She

imagined the truck driver stepping out to survey the damage and the beast attacking him too. It would go after anyone who got in the way of its hunt.

Yeah, you can't count on anyone to save you but you. Until you get to a phone and call for help, you won't be safe.

Melanie marched on, hoping this dirt road would lead to a home or a convenience store. If nothing else, it should join with the main highway at some point, which would lead to the visitor center.

What if it does join with the highway but after the visitor center and you pass it without knowing it?

She shook her head. She couldn't afford to think negative thoughts at a time like this. When her life was so full of negativity, she had to force herself to believe good things would come.

This trail will lead right to the visitor center. It'll be less than a mile away. No sweat.

In fact, even better, it'll lead to a police station. That's where it will lead. Right into the arms of law enforcement officials.

A slight whimper escaped her lips as she limped along the road. Her knees ached and so did her right ankle. She hadn't broken anything, but everything was bruised and battered. Adrenaline might have masked some of the pain earlier, but it was wearing off. She'd been through two accidents. Her body had been put through the wringer. It occurred to her as she whined that she was the only thing making noise.

The woods should have been alive with crickets and birds and frogs. This was West Virginia. The nights were always alive with nature's symphony. This wasn't right.

It reminded her of stories her cousin Torie used to tell about Harmony Holler. It was called that because nothing was harmonious about it. A witch lived there and was said to make stews out of the county's orphans. Melanie never believed the stories, but she'd always remembered the part about the woods in the holler being dead silent because the insects and animals knew better than to travel to those parts. When an area was truly evil, critters sensed it and steered clear.

Are the critters steering clear from here now?

She couldn't remember hearing anything up near the highway either. Then again, she'd been with friends, and they'd all been fleeing for their lives. They hadn't stopped long enough to listen.

ROAD WRATH

Now that she was alone, it was clear she was absolutely *alone*.

Melanie paused to look back toward the van sitting against the tree at the cliff's edge. It seemed safer back there for some reason. She considered turning back, but if nobody came for her, she could be there forever, or at least until the sun came up and baked her. Or until she gave up altogether and dove off the mountain.

She turned once more and peered into the darkness of the woods. She knew nothing about what lay ahead in that direction.

If you have faith as small as a mustard seed . . .

Squaring her shoulders, Melanie took a deep breath and continued. Whatever was going to come her way would come whether she shriveled in fear or stood strong and pushed onward. So, she walked.

Her phone was gone, lost during the wreck in the van, so she had no idea how long she'd walked or what time it was, but it felt like she'd been walking for hours when she heard organ music cutting through the silence.

Melanie stopped and focused on the sound.

At first, she thought her mind was playing tricks on her. Sometimes in moments of silence—like when dipping her head under the lake—her mind conjured new sounds to replace nonexistent ones. After listening for a full minute, she was sure this music was real, and it was coming from up ahead.

She moved to the edge of the road, hiding among the trees as she crept forward. The last time she'd heard music that came anywhere close to what she was hearing now, it was flowing from speakers inside the pickup truck of the old couple parked outside the visitor center. The same old couple who'd run them off the highway.

After the night she'd been through, she was no longer afraid of bumping into them. In fact, she kind of hoped she'd have the chance to exact revenge on the two old bastards for what had happened to her friends.

She may not be able to go toe-to-toe with the big creature that stalked them all night, but she could handle the frail old couple.

The music led her onward until she rounded a bend and saw a faint light in the distance. It appeared to be a porch light, and as Melanie came closer, she saw that it illuminated the front of an old church painted a dark brown.

An old, rusty tractor sat broke down in the front yard. Next to it was a rusted jungle gym and a swing set with one swing. One of its chains had snapped in half and dangled to the ground. This was a family church, but it didn't look like kids had played on that lawn in a long time.

No cars were parked in the dirt lot out front. As Melanie stepped closer to the entrance, she saw that the small sign out front read: Church of Hezekiah Downs.

Under that read: An eternity in Hellwater ain't so long when you've prepared for it. – Father Hezekiah.

Under that read: Rotters smell like bacon when turned on a spit. Who doesn't love bacon? – Father Hezekiah.

To the left of the text was a strange symbol that looked like a frown, but each end was an arrow, and up near the curved top of the frown were two parallel lines crossing through it that made it kind of look like the letter "H." It was a strange, creepy symbol, and Melanie was sure she'd seen it somewhere before.

Melanie felt the hairs on the back of her neck stand up as she read the sign quotes. She remembered the old man's words when he'd asked her if she knew what the Book of Hezekiah said about friends. She had no doubt this Book of Hezekiah came from this church, and if it came from this church, she had no desire to enter through these doors.

Yet it might be the only place around with a phone.

The organ music playing from inside was a fresh reminder that someone was inside. Nobody sharing a religion with that creepy old couple could be friendly. Still, Melanie didn't know what else to do. It could be a long walk to the next phone. But what if they left the music always playing? It was possible. Doubtful, but possible.

There were no cars outside and it didn't appear to have a house attached. Unless somebody lived inside the building, the place might have been empty.

She couldn't believe she was about to do this. Light shone from underneath the main chapel doors so she knew the spotlight would be on her the moment she entered. There'd be no sneaking in under the cover of darkness. It was risky, but rather than creep around the sides and try to find a secret door, she decided to walk right through the main entrance where nobody would expect her.

The doors swung outward with a loud squeak, and she winced as the bright light blasted her face. She rubbed her eyes and squinted as she peered inside.

Inside was void of human life. Music played loudly but nobody was there staring at her or waiting to call her out for interrupting the service. She wasn't about to be sacrificed to some dark god for barging in on mass. The relief that washed over her was almost overwhelming. Melanie nearly fell into the first pew as she thanked God for this blessing.

She didn't allow herself to sit long. If this was the old couple's place of worship, they'd turn up eventually, and when they did, she needed to be long gone. There was no telling what they'd do if they found her there and who knew how crazy the rest of their cult members were.

Melanie made her way down the center aisle and toward the back of the church. As she did, she couldn't help comparing what she saw to her church. In place of copies of the *Holy Bible* that were always available where she worshipped, there were black books embossed with the symbol she'd seen on the sign out front.

The room was decorated in black and red. Instead of depictions of Jesus Christ, his miracles, blessings, and other positive messages about everlasting life, God's grace, and the Kingdom of Heaven, this church decorated its walls with blasphemous imagery, gruesome deaths, and illustrations of mass destruction. Horrifying deaths taking place around the world were displayed in gory detail. Melanie's stomach turned as she looked at the walls, and she had to focus on the floor to make it through the building.

At the rear was a door. She was careful as she entered, unsure of what she'd find on the other side. All she needed was to interrupt a ritual taking place in one of the back rooms.

The door was quiet when she opened it, not that it would matter since the music in the other room played so loudly it would mask any noise she was likely to make. Still, it felt necessary to remain quiet. The next room was a cold, dank, cinderblock room. No phone.

"You've got to be kidding me. Come on."

She backed out and when she turned, she saw the old man from the visitor center standing near the church's main doors. He had his hands on his hips and was staring at her, shaking his head and grinning. He sucked on his teeth and said something she couldn't hear over the loud music.

Melanie's heart dropped. As much as she'd wanted to get

revenge on the old couple, seeing this man again struck fear in her like she hadn't expected.

His mouth moved again but she couldn't hear his words.

"What?!" she replied. "I can't hear you."

If she couldn't hear him, she knew he wouldn't be able to hear her either.

She stepped closer to him but only a few steps.

His mouth moved again but still she couldn't make out the words.

"I said I can't hear you!" she replied.

He tried once more.

"I can't," she began with her words drowned out by the music, but then the music shut off and the room went silent, so her words came out in a shout as she finished with, "hear you!"

Melanie's head whipped around, and she saw the old woman behind her, fiddling with the organ. She'd turned the music off, plunging the room into silence.

"Bet you can fucking hear me now!" the old man shouted.

"Is that better, dear?" the old lady asked.

"I think it is much better," the old man said.

"I think so, too," the old lady said.

Melanie stepped to the side, moving away from the center aisle so she could put her back against the wall. She didn't trust that someone else wouldn't figure out a way to sneak up on her. This way she could see to her left and right. If anyone else came towards her, she'd know it.

"Now, as I was saying," the old man said, "oh, here you are."

The old woman giggled. "Oh, here she is."

"Here she is," the old man repeated.

"Here she is," the old woman sang.

They seemed to be having fun with this. Of course, they would. They were winning whatever game this was. All of Melanie's friends were dead—and over what? Because there'd been some disrespectful words exchanged at the visitor center? Or because the old lady had wanted a cigarette, and nobody had given her one? Melanie still wasn't sure what had started them down this path.

Because there wasn't a reason. People like this don't need a reason. Evil is evil, pure and simple. They do evil things because they can.

"We thought we'd lost you for a little while," the old man added. "You were so helpful back there at the candy machine. Did you know, dear, she offered to help me purchase candy?"

The old lady scowled. "The tramp."

The old man laughed. "No, not like that."

"Not like what?" the old lady asked. "The little hussy thinks she can offer my man some of her sweet little candy?"

The old man laughed more. "You're such a jealous one. It's only your candy I want, dear."

"That's right," the old woman said, hiking up her dress to display herself. She wasn't wearing any underwear and her hairy mound was on full display. Melanie would have looked away if it hadn't happened so quickly. "You can have all my candy your heart desires. But only my candy. No other twat's Skittles or Jujubes."

"Only yours," the old man promised.

The old lady ran two fingers up her slit and then flicked them in the old man's direction. He opened his mouth and licked the air like a dog eagerly lapping up water.

"Mmm mmm . . . damn you got the good puddin'!" the old man shouted.

The old woman cackled and dropped her dress.

Melanie was about to throw up in her mouth.

"You're meant for each other," Melanie said. "I don't want any of it. Can you just let me go now?"

"Let you go?" the old lady asked. "Why, of course not. You've been marked. Wrath will be upon you."

"Is that what that thing is out there?" Melanie asked. "That creature?"

The old lady gasped and slapped a hand over her heart. "Creature?"

"Oh, you shouldn't have said that," the old man said.

As the couple talked, Melanie shifted her gaze to the right, where the old man stood blocking the door, over to her left where the old woman had stepped down from the organ onto the main stage.

"Beast, then?" Melanie replied.

"Beast?" the old lady asked, shocked. "How dare you?"

"What would you call it then?" Melanie replied.

"Our boy," the old man said.

"My pride and joy," the old lady answered.

"I don't understand," Melanie said. As she listened, she searched the floor for anything she might use as a weapon. The only thing was a collection basket at the end of a long wooden pole. That pole would have to work.

"Of course you don't," the old lady replied. "How could you? You're just a young slut out there spreadin' your legs for who knows who. You ain't had no little-uns of your own."

"It's your baby?" Melanie asked.

"My first and only son," the old woman said proudly. "First and only child at all!"

Melanie's eyes shot open. She couldn't believe that warped, mangled monster she'd seen on the highway—that demonic thing that ate her friends, ripped into her boyfriend with its teeth, and sucked Sean's bones dry—was this couple's baby boy.

"When you're asked to give the ultimate sacrifice to the one and only god that matters and Father Hezekiah blesses you in the way that we've been blessed . . . oh, child." The old woman closed her eyes and inhaled a long breath as if accepting a fresh new blessing from their evil lord. "Don't you see? We travel around now with our very own son of wrath in our camper and send him after anyone deserving of his rage."

"Each death is a sacrifice," the old man said.

"And each sacrifice is good," the old woman added.

"See? We're favored by Father Hezekiah and the dark lord himself. Because we find little pansies like your friends and you," the old man said.

"Perfect sacrifices," the old woman added. "Keeps the dark lord happy with our congregation. Keeps him satisfied with us all."

Melanie thought about the creature's face and how it resembled that of a baby boy, like a small, chubby-faced child. It looked that way because it had been a child before transforming into the disgusting monster it was now. These evil bastards had turned their son into a monster. They deserved to rot in Hell. As the sign out front said, 'An eternity in hellwater.' She hoped they bathed in it forever.

"That's sick," Melanie said. "You're both sick."

The old lady glared with the fire of pure hatred blazing in her eyes.

"You're so lucky our congregation is asleep right now or you'd have eighty angry souls seeking vengeance on you for your vile words!"

ROAD WRATH

"Go to Hell!" Melanie declared. "Both of you. Take your demon child and your eighty angry assholes with you!"

The old man stumbled up one of the rows and came around the corner while her attention was on the old woman. He'd snuck up on her. He pulled out his razor wire whip and was moving closer when Melanie ducked and came back up with the wooden pole. She swung it hard and clocked him on the jaw. The old man went down hard, falling and smacking his head on one of the benches.

Melanie had expected the old woman to charge after her, but instead, she went to her husband's aid and knelt next to him to ensure he was okay.

Melanie hobbled outside as quickly as she could, ditching the pole because it was too long and odd to carry. She saw the camper and the pickup truck. She moved around to the driver's side, climbed inside, and searched for the keys. They were nowhere in sight.

"Seriously?"

She'd hoped the old man would have put the keys in the visor or kept them in the ignition, but she should have known better. They were probably in his pocket or his wife's possession.

Melanie was about to get out of the truck when she looked in the passenger seat and saw the Polaroid pictures of her friends and her. She scooped them up and took a closer look. In all the pictures, there was a reddish circle drawn around each of them. Melanie let her fingers run over the photos. The red circles had texture to them. She scraped at one of them with her finger and some of it came off and got stuck under her fingernail.

"Is this . . . blood? What the hell?"

Looking at the photos again she saw Sean, Ansley, Tucker, and Rowena all had the red circles drawn around them. So did hers.

Is this how they're sending the creature after us?

She remembered the bandages on the old woman's fingers. It was her blood. She was circling the photos.

And what if I scratch away the circle around my head? What if I can remove the circle from my picture? Would that unmark me?

Using her fingernail, she scraped at the caked-on blood and watched it begin to chip away. She wasn't sure if she could get all the blood off the photograph, but it seemed possible.

Inside the church, the old lady screamed in pure raw rage. They would be coming soon, and they would be searching for Melanie.

She had to get rid of the circle while she escaped. She shoved the photos into her pocket, all except hers, and disappeared into the dark forest.

CHAPTER 9

MELANIE USED HER thumbnail to scratch at the circle around her head until she was sure she'd gotten most of the dried blood off the picture. At least as far as she could tell by feeling along the photo's smooth surface. The gritty texture of the blood seemed to be gone but she couldn't see well in the dark. She was sure she must have rubbed her face off the picture, too.

She wondered what that would do. Would erasing her from the photo change anything? For that matter, would getting rid of the photo stop the curse? What if she ripped it up into tiny pieces or burned it?

What if she ran all the way back to the van and Frisbee-flung the damn thing off the side of the mountain?

These were her thoughts as she moved as quickly as she could through the dark woods, making sure she could see the dirt road at all times so she wouldn't get lost. She'd been walking about fifteen minutes when she heard that demented choir music floating on the wind followed by the rumble of the old pickup's engine.

Melanie squatted down in the brush but didn't think they'd see her at the speed they were traveling down the dirt road. They wouldn't hear her either with their music turned up so loud. Plus, the squeaking of the rickety camper in tow covered any noise she made. She could have sneezed or even stood up and yelled, 'I'm over here!' It wouldn't have mattered.

They weren't searching for her, and she knew why. They were content their son, their demon kid, would hunt her down.

Surely, they'd noticed the photos were missing, which meant they didn't care that the pictures were gone. They didn't believe Melanie could stop the Wrath curse.

This worried her. If they weren't concerned about it, then

maybe Melanie had been wrong about erasing the bloody circle. Maybe the monster still searched for her.

No, you're okay. If that thing was still hunting you, it would have found you by now.

A branch cracked somewhere deep in the forest, and Melanie froze. It was the only sound other than any she'd made herself that she could remember since entering the woods. The area's wildlife had remained silent. Its creatures wanted nothing to do with the Church of Hezekiah Downs or the land around it.

The wind blew through the trees, and they swooshed overhead, causing another branch to crack.

It's only the wind. You're okay.

She was jumpy. She needed to get the hell out of this forest. Now that the truck had passed, she could walk on the dirt road again. If the old couple returned, she'd hear them long before they got close enough. Her aching feet and tired muscles would appreciate flatter ground.

Thirty minutes on the dirt road saw her much farther along than her trek through the trees would have allowed. At the end of the painful hour hike, she saw the highway up ahead, and she was grateful to be leaving this hidden back road. Her swan dive off the mountain had left her feeling like she'd dropped down a hellbilly rabbit hole a mile from Hades.

Melanie had lived in West Virginia all her life and had never traveled down a back road that led to a dark church like that Church of Hezekiah Downs. That place needed to be knocked off the map.

At least now she knew no matter how long it took, if she kept walking, she would make it to civilization. It was out there somewhere. *Home* was only so far away.

When Melanie reached the highway, she stretched her arms toward the sky and closed her eyes for a moment in quiet celebration.

"I'm closer. I'm gonna make it."

She didn't feel so helpless. Things got even better when she opened her eyes and started walking in the direction of home only to see the sign that read: Rest Area 1 Mile.

The Visitor Center. Only one mile? I can make that. Only one mile!

Looking behind, she thought about her boyfriend's severed

head lying on the highway somewhere back there and his wrecked SUV abandoned on the roadside. Sean, Ansley, Rowena—even Mike who'd been sweet enough to pull over and try to help them— were all dead back there, but she was still alive. She would make it because they couldn't.

"One mile to go, girl. You got this."

And she walked.

She'd heard the average person walked a fifteen-minute mile. This final lap of hers seemed to take so much longer. That probably had a lot to do with her battered body. She was afraid to see what she looked like in a mirror and vowed to stay strong when she saw her reflection in the ones hanging above the sinks in the visitor center bathroom.

The thought of running cool water over her face excited her and made her walk faster. She was so thirsty she'd lap up the sink water or might even find something to smash open one of the soda machines in the snack shack.

"Do you need some help making a purchase from the machine?"

Thinking of the snack machine reminded her of the old man. Why had she offered him help? It seemed like that was the moment this all started. If she'd walked out of the building without talking to the old man, would all of this have happened?

Yes, it would have because that had nothing to do with it. It started with the old woman asking for a cigarette.

Melanie remembered every detail of that first confrontation. She wondered how many others had bumped into the old couple on road trips. Had they sent their demonic child after other travelers or was this all a fluke? Was this their first time? She doubted that. They were so quick to run the SUV off the road, like they'd done it a hundred times before.

They have to be stopped. It, the beast, must be stopped. But how?

Random thoughts occupied her mind until she could see the visitor center ahead. She'd gone to so many of her high school football games and thought the distance looked about the length of the football field. A hundred yards and she'd be there.

Melanie saw headlights on the opposite side of the highway and wondered if she should try to flag the driver for help. The last time she'd done that, the poor guy ended up dead, flung off the side of the mountain. She doubted she could get the driver's attention anyway from where she was. They were way over on the other side of the highway.

The vehicle seemed to be slowing without any effort on her part to signal them.

It was the engine rattle that caught her attention next. Even from far away, she knew it was the familiar rumble of the old pickup.

The wicked old couple was on the other side of the highway, driving toward her, and they'd spotted her. The old man would be driving. He was always driving, and he'd brought the truck to an almost complete stop as if he was contemplating whether he should get out and cross the highway on foot.

Lucky for Melanie, this part of the highway had a median separating it. Guardrails and a gulch of grass between them kept the old man from swinging the truck around and barreling toward her.

Melanie picked up her pace the best she could.

The truck's horn honked once and Melanie understood it as the old man's way of yelling, 'Dammit!'

The pickup sped off toward the next turnabout. Melanie had no idea how far away that was, so she didn't know how much time she had. She did know what it would mean for her if she didn't get to that visitor center and behind closed doors before the old couple caught up with her.

Her breaths came in heavy gasps and sweat dripped down her forehead as she fought through pain and exhaustion to get to her destination. She allowed herself a couple of quick glances over her shoulder to see if the truck was behind her. Each time she checked, she saw no headlights. That luck would run out soon enough.

As her feet moved along the side of the highway, stepping over cracked asphalt and weeds, her thumb continued to rub at her photograph. By now, the circle of blood that had once wound around her face wasn't there at all. It had to be the reason the creature hadn't shown up to devour her.

The trees to Melanie's right lit up in a yellowish cone that shone against her back and cast a shadow in front of her. The pickup was behind her. It was still far back there, but it was approaching fast.

Melanie reached the sidewalk that lined the visitor center parking lot. She cut across the grass and ran past the picnic tables. She wanted as many obstacles between her and the truck as possible.

They may catch up with her, but they couldn't run her over.

Those old bastards would have to get out of the truck and come get her. At least on foot, she stood a chance against the creeps.

Melanie's chest burned. She'd never moved so fast and with such purpose in all her life.

The visitor center doors were only a few feet ahead. She glanced left and saw the pickup park at the center of the parking lot. No other cars were around.

With the doors so close, Melanie was almost afraid to touch them. If she tried and they wouldn't open, she wouldn't know what to do. She needed the doors to be unlocked.

"Please, God. Please let the doors be unlocked."

She reached the doors and shoved one of them inward. It swung open so smoothly that she nearly tripped and fell. A cool blast of air-conditioned air hit her.

"Hello?!" she called.

Nobody answered. She looked to the parking lot and saw the old man exiting the truck. He didn't seem in a rush as he fumbled with his belt buckle and adjusted his pants.

"Hello?" Melanie tried again. "Mitch?"

Still no reply.

She saw an office door next to the men's room. She tried the knob and found it locked. She banged on it with a closed fist. "Hello? Mitch!"

"Hey . . . hang on," a man's voice came from the other side of the door.

The door popped open, and Mitch stood there wiping the sleep from his eyes.

"Can . . . can I hel . . . help you?" he asked.

"Mitch," Melanie said.

He squinted and gave her a once-over. "Ya . . . yeah. Who . . . who are . . . " He stopped talking and snapped his fingers. "Wait a . . . a . . . a ma . . . minute. You."

"You remember me?" Melanie asked.

He nodded. "Wha . . . what happened to you?"

"Your friends," she told him. "That crazy old couple did this. Do you have a phone in there?"

He nodded again.

"Good. Move out of the way. I need to call for help."

He shook his head.

"Mitch, move. Please."

"It wa . . . won't work. Not while the ca . . . curse is on. Na . . . no phones will."

Melanie's heart dropped. She'd been trying to reach this place all night so she could make a single phone call and Mitch was saying it had all been for nothing.

"If I can't call for help then . . . Mitch, how do I end this?"

Mitch shook his head and raised his hand to scratch his chin in thought. When he did, the sleeve of his shirt fell from his wrist, and Melanie got a closer look at the tattoos she'd seen earlier that day. This time she got a clear view of one in particular. It was familiar. It resembled a frown but with arrows at the ends, pointing down, and up at the center of the frown were two parallel lines cutting through it to make it look like the letter H.

It was the symbol from the church sign.

"The Church of Hezekiah Downs," she said. "You're one of them."

Mitch saw what she'd zeroed in on and frantically shook his head. "Na . . . na . . . no. That's oh . . . oh . . . old. This one's new." He lifted his other sleeve and showed Melanie the Christian sign of the cross.

She didn't know if she should believe it. Could she trust him? What if he was lying and it was the other way around? What if he was once a Christian and was now a follower of that Hezekiah fellow?

"How do I know?" Melanie said, backing away.

She hadn't heard the old man enter the visitor center. When she turned to flee from Mitch, she ran right into the old bastard.

The old man laughed and nearly lost his splintered false teeth in the process. He caught them and stuffed them back in his mouth.

"Mitch," he said. "Good to see you, son."

"Ma . . . Mr. Clem," Mitch said. "What's ga . . . ga . . . going on here?"

"Almost lost us a good one," Clem said. "Kind of like we lost you. Would be good if you come back to mass again."

"Na . . . no. And no for her ta . . . too. You la . . . let her go."

"Mitch, you'd be better off minding your business if you know—"

"La . . . let her go!" Mitch yelled as he brought a heavy closed fist down on the crown of Clem's head.

Clem stumbled backward, stunned as he dropped to one knee.

Melanie had a moment to slip away. She was about to run outside when she saw the old woman approaching the doors.

Mitch looked through the doors, then looked at Melanie. "Ha . . . hide."

He stepped into the office, and it sounded like he was flipping a few switches. The interior of the visitor center went dark.

Melanie hadn't had a chance to hide, so she crouched behind a newspaper rack. From there, she watched and listened as Mitch and Clem argued.

"Turn the lights back on, boy!" Clem demanded.

"Ga . . . go away!" Mitch ordered.

"Turn the lights on so I can find that little hussy!"

"No! Ga . . . go!"

"I said turn them damn lights back on, you fuckin' retard!"

With dim light from outside shining through the glass doors, Melanie saw Clem pull out his razor wire weapon, hold it high, and swing it down at Mitch's shoulder and neck. It tore into the big man's flesh and ripped out a chunk of meat.

Mitch screamed.

Clem laughed and danced a little jig.

"Yeehaw, boy!" Clem yelled. "Want another?!"

"Na . . . no," Mitch said, his voice much lower this time. He sounded defeated, and Melanie was worried he'd give up and help the old couple catch her.

"Then turn them fucking lights on right this instant before my lovely wife gets in here and has to make her way through the fucking dark."

"No!" Mitch yelled.

"No?" Clem asked.

"Na . . . no!" Mitch answered. "I said na . . . no! Go! Ga . . . get out!"

Clem cackled and raised his razor wire again. He was about to bring it down when Mitch roared, ran at the frail old man, and football tackled him. The big man lifted Clem high into the air, ran toward the doors, and drove him through the glass. The sound of exploding glass was so loud that Melanie flinched in her hiding spot.

Mitch landed on top of the old man, and with his wife watching in horror, the big man raised both his fists and brought them down on Clem's face over and over. "I said go!"

It looked like a gorilla smashing the face of a helpless old man.

"No!" the old woman screamed. "Clem!"

Melanie watched in stunned silence.

"I said ga . . . go," Mitch said one final time as he rolled off the old man.

"Clem?" the old woman asked as she inched forward, afraid to come too close to Mitch.

Mitch crawled on his hands and knees through the broken doors and collapsed onto his stomach in the middle of all the shattered glass.

Behind him, the old woman crept toward her husband. Her hands shook as she collapsed to her knees at his side and gripped his shirt in both hands.

Mitch didn't know where Melanie was hiding, but he forced one word out over the broken glass acting as his pillow. "Ra . . . run."

The old woman was already back to her feet, leaning forward as she stalked her prey, pointing a long and crooked finger at the darkness inside the visitor center.

"I know you're in there you wicked little cunt, and you're gonna pay for this."

Melanie hid behind the newspaper rack, watching as the old woman stalked toward the women's bathroom. With her back turned it was the perfect moment to attack.

Remaining hunched over, Melanie waddled closer, trying her best to stay quiet on knees that ached, thighs that burned, and an ankle that felt like it wanted to snap and keep her there at the visitor center forever. Each step made her want to scream.

Now was the point where she could either dash for the doors or run straight at the old hag and perform the same move Mitch did on her husband. She could drive her right into the brick wall.

Doubt set in and Melanie wondered if she had the skill or the strength to pull it off.

She glanced over at Mitch and saw him watching her through heavy eyelids that blinked slowly, looking like they wanted to close forever. He seemed to understand what she was thinking and tried to shake his head. He wanted her to go. To save herself. To run.

The old woman still had her back turned.

"Hiding out in the poop shoot, are ya?" she called. "I bet you's in the little boys' room though aintcha? Yeah, you're the type to flash your little snatch all over the boys' room."

Yes, keep heading that way, you old witch. Keep talking trash, too.
Melanie decided she was going to tackle the old bitch. It was now or never.

The old lady wheeled around. "Gotcha!"

The room was illuminated with a quick shot of brightness that blinded Melanie and caused her to throw her hands up in front of her face to shield herself. "Take that, ya filthy twat!" the old lady added as she slashed out with her husband's razor wire weapon, tearing a gash across Melanie's hands.

Melanie screamed and fell on her ass. Blood ran down her palms and she couldn't see a thing.

The old woman had used the Polaroid camera to blind her.

"How did that feel?" the old woman taunted. "Care for another?"

It hurt like hell but didn't seem to dig too deeply into her hands.

"Please," Melanie begged. "Please don't hurt me."

Begging wasn't in her nature, but she needed to buy some time because she couldn't see a thing. The old lady laughed and that was good. Anything other than hitting her again with that vicious tool she wielded was good.

"Oh, I'm gonna hurt you, girl!" the old lady hollered.

"He . . . here," Mitch yelled and slid a large piece of glass from the broken door over to Melanie.

Her vision was clear enough, so she snatched it up and drove it into the old woman's foot. She howled in pain and dropped the camera.

Melanie caught it and crawled toward the door.

As she made her escape, a sound echoed in the distance that made her freeze and nearly piss herself—a loud childlike laughter that turned into a cackle and a roar. She'd heard that sound before when the beast was ripping into Tucker on the highway.

Behind her, the old woman's cry of agony turned into one of great joy. She laughed and clapped her hands together.

"That's right, girlie! You better run! My son is coming! And he's not gonna be happy his daddy's gone! You're already cursed. And, oh, the things he's gonna do to you!"

Melanie turned and limped out the door, looking once at Mitch, hoping he would be okay.

CHAPTER 10

THE BEAST'S CALLS echoed off the mountain walls and tormented Melanie as she left the visitor center and searched for a hiding place. She had no place to go. If it was coming for her, it was going to come no matter where she went. The old couple's pickup and camper was parked in the middle of the parking lot. It was as good a place as any to hide. Maybe the monster wouldn't think to look for her in its home.

As she expected, the camper door was unlocked. The old couple wasn't afraid of anyone breaking into it. Anyone foolish enough to try would run right into the arms of their devil child.

Here she was, stepping into its lair with no assurance she'd ever exit. When the door swung outward, she heard the clatter of dry bones dangling like those beaded curtains popular in the seventies and eighties. She wasn't surprised by it.

What caught her off-guard was the pungent odor of wet animal. It reminded her of Ansley's dog. Her family never bathed it enough and it always had a musky scent. The room reeked of that mixed with human body odor, piss, shit, and a somewhat sweet scent that she thought might have been decaying meat.

To the left was a large cage that took up most of the space in the camper. A circular red and green rug was on the floor of the cage. Chew toys mangled beyond repair lay all over it.

In one corner lay a piece of newspaper with a rather large, swirled pile of shit sitting on it. A few other chunks of feces were scattered about on the classifieds section as well. Melanie covered her nose and mouth to keep from hurling.

A black and white TV, a VCR, and a VHS tape rewinder sat on an old dresser beyond the cage. There were stacks of all the seasons of *Little House on the Prairie* along with several *Faces of Death* videos, all the seasons of *Friday the 13th: The Series,* and the animated series *Adventures of the Gummi Bears.*

"No wonder he's so violent," Melanie said as she took in her surroundings.

To the right of the entertainment area was what could be considered the old woman's entertainment area. It was clearly where she performed her black magic. There was a countertop with a shelf full of boxes and jars with handwritten labels marking the contents.

Outside the camper, the sound of the beast grew louder. Its growl was close. Melanie turned toward the door and locked it just as the creature smashed into it. The strike was so hard she thought it might blow the door right off its hinges. There was heavy breathing as it backed away from the camper.

All was quiet for a moment.

She could hear the thing outside moving around, but it wasn't attacking.

Had she been right about removing the circle of blood around her picture?

Her excitement was short-lived. The beast rammed into the camper so hard it tilted and slammed back down on its tires. Melanie yelped and grabbed hold of the counter, holding on for dear life as the camper shook wildly. The creature thrashed around outside. She'd been wrong about the picture. It wanted her. It still wanted to kill her like all the others.

The beast was throwing a temper tantrum outside like a small child, and Melanie had no doubt it would get in the camper soon enough.

I'm going to die here.

Panic set in. She thought she was strong. She thought she could do this, but she'd been wrong. She was going to die in this gross camper.

This isn't how I want to die.

The camper tilted and rocked.

One of the windows crashed inward. Glass blew all over the place and against the cage.

The window closest to Melanie smashed inward and tiny shards nicked her skin.

She screamed.

"Stop it!" she yelled. "Leave me alone!"

The creature shrieked and then giggled like a child.

"Stop it!" it mimicked. "Leave me alone!" It laughed again.

Melanie's face grew beet red.

"Let me in," the beast said in the same childlike voice.

Melanie set the camera down on the counter and reached into her pocket to pull out the picture of herself the old woman had taken. She'd rubbed at the circle of blood the entire time she'd walked to the visitor center, but she'd done it all in the dark. Now, as she looked at it in the light of the camper, she saw that she'd missed some of the circle. She hadn't rubbed it all off. There was still some dried blood around her head.

"Go to hell," Melanie whispered.

"Go to hell," it mimicked. "Let's go to hell together." Melanie ignored it. "Let me in. Open the door and I'll only eat your insides."

Melanie used her fingernail to scratch at the circle.

The beast slammed its body against the door as if it knew what she was doing.

As the final piece of the bloody ring disappeared from around her head, the beast's shaking ceased.

Melanie waited and listened as the creature backed away. It sounded like it might be whining, complaining like a small child who'd had its toy taken away.

Melanie laughed quietly. She couldn't believe it.

Is it possible?

There was no more shaking at the door. No more pounding. The beast's cackling was gone.

"Truly I tell you. If you have faith as small as a mustard seed . . . "

Melanie was still facing the counter full of the old witch's materials. She saw containers with weird stuff like rattlesnake venom, crow feet, toenail clippings, and pig snout. She saw sickening ingredients like "the blood of the forgotten child", "twice regurgitated intestine", and "the left eye of that one hippie". She even saw mundane elements like cayenne pepper, sage, and paprika. One item on that shelf made her stop, grin, and look up at the ceiling.

"Mustard seed," she read as she picked up the fist-sized glass jar. It was filled with tiny seeds. "You've got to be kidding me."

It was poetic and perfect. She quickly formulated a plan.

First, she needed a weapon.

A baseball bat, a broomstick, a—

Melanie spotted a rusty toolbox on the floor beneath the counter. Inside was a heavy metal wrench.

Nice.

If her hands were full, she wouldn't be able to hold the camera. On the counter, she found a spool of twine. She looked toward the door and saw the bone curtain she'd passed through when entering. It was the twine holding the bones together. Melanie used a piece of glass from one of the shattered windows to cut a piece of twine from the spool. She tied it to both ends of the camera so it could hang around her neck.

Melanie stepped carefully and quietly out of the camper, half expecting the beast to drop down from the roof or come whipping around from the back, but it didn't.

All was silent outside.

Unnervingly quiet, until the old woman's vile voice sliced through the soundless dread.

"What is this tomfoolery?"

She sat at one of the picnic tables between the visitor center doors and the snack shack. She'd found the cigarette she'd wanted earlier that day. The cigarette that started this whole ordeal. This one looked like she'd rolled it herself. It was nearly black. She sucked on it, making one end light up in the night.

A thin ribbon of smoke seeped out of her nostrils and dissipated in the air. Melanie thought the old woman, with all her voodoo bullshit inside the camper, could probably make that tendril of smoke dance for her if she wanted.

"You should be ripped to ribbons by now," the old woman said.

"Seems your son has a thing for brunettes," Melanie said as she walked toward the old woman with both hands behind her back.

The old woman stood from her seated position, flicked her cigarette into the parking lot, and limped toward Melanie. "You've proven yourself quite the adversary. Maybe you should join the church."

"I've seen your church, and I'm not impressed."

The old woman let the razor wire dangle from her fist. "You've seen nothing."

Melanie laughed. "We don't worship the same God."

"Of course. we don't. Mine takes me places."

"Oh, he's going to all right."

They continued to approach each other. When she was ten feet away, the old woman stopped and cocked her head, studying Melanie. "What you got there behind your back, missy?"

"Nothing much. Just something of yours I found inside the camper. Thought you might want it back."

Melanie took a couple more steps forward, mindful that the old woman could whip that razor wire out at any second. She needed to stay out of reach.

"And what might that be?" the old lady asked.

"It's one of your ingredients," Melanie said.

It was clear she'd piqued the old woman's interest.

"And it's how I hold power over you, your demon son, and everything having to do with your worthless church."

The old woman's eyes opened wide, and her saggy jowls shook with fury.

Melanie pulled her left hand from behind her back and held up the jar of mustard seeds.

The old woman laughed. "What the hell is that?"

Melanie handed it to her and much to her surprise, the old woman brought up her razor wire wielding hand to accept it, holding the jar between her thumb and middle fingers while the leather handle of the weapon dangled loosely.

The old woman held the jar up in front of her eyes, a few inches from her face, and read from the label. "Mustard seeds?"

"If I only needed faith as small as a mustard seed," Melanie said, "imagine what I can do with all this faith."

Melanie swung the metal wrench with her right hand and smashed the jar. It exploded, sending pieces of jagged glass into the old woman's face and eyes. The old lady howled in agony as the wrench continued, striking her between the eyes. She fell to her knees and dropped the razor wire.

Melanie kicked the weapon into the parking lot, far from the old lady's reach. The woman brought both hands to her face, trying to claw out the pieces of jagged glass in her cheeks, forehead, and nose. One large shard had slammed into her right eyeball.

Melanie tucked the wrench into the back of her pants, lifted the camera hanging from her neck, and pointed it at the old woman.

"I didn't ask for this," Melanie told her. "None of my friends did. You did this. You did all of this. You and your evil—"

"You are fucking dead!" the old woman yelled.

"Someday," Melanie replied. "Sure. But not today."

The old woman screamed obscenities and writhed in pain. Melanie snapped a picture and quickly dipped her fingers in the woman's bloody wounds.

Melanie shook the picture and watched the image come to life. She had to fight back the urge to laugh at the old woman's wild photo. With her fingers still slathered in the old woman's blood, she circled the photo with it and tossed it out into the parking lot.

Within seconds, the beast's cackle sounded off from within the trees. He was still out there roaming free in the woods. Now, he was on the hunt again, pursuing the cursed person in the photo.

Stalking his mother.

"Baby?" the old woman asked, instantly stopping her screaming.

She had her right eye closed. Blood ran down from its corner. The other was wide open and looking toward the trees. Blood ran from other gashes in her face temporarily blinding her. She wasn't going to die from those cuts. Not even close. Melanie knew she'd only injured the woman. She might lose that eye but other than that, she would have been fine.

But there was no coming back from what the beast was about to do to her.

She hoped.

The thing emerged from the trees on all fours and Melanie backed up to the camper. It didn't run at her the way it had come at Melanie's friends. It didn't scale the mountain walls or leap from the trees. It moved methodically, almost like it wasn't sure it was doing the right thing.

"Baby," the old woman said. "It's Momma."

"Mommy," the beast said in its creepy, childlike voice. "Mommy, that's you?"

"Yes, baby. It's your Momma. Everything will be okay. Let's get you back into your room in the camper."

The beast growled. It didn't like that idea.

"Or better yet," the old woman said. "Maybe you'd like another snack. Right over there." The old woman pointed at Melanie.

The thing continued toward its mother and didn't even look Melanie's way.

"Over there, baby," the old woman tried again.

The beast continued forward.

"Do you hear me, baby?" she asked.

The beast cackled and growled. It was drawn toward its mother. The curse was too strong. Whatever dark magic the old woman had constructed with the blood and the photos was pulling it toward her and no amount of talking would get her out of it. It had no interest in Melanie.

"Baby, please," the old woman said.

It growled once more and took off running at her.

The old woman screamed.

It pounced and landed on her, tearing with its teeth and claws.

Melanie was stunned, staring at the scene in utter shock.

The beast was chewing on its mother, and this looked more like the blood and guts Melanie was used to seeing in horror movies. The old woman's skin seemed to stretch and break apart in the creature's mouth. Her intestines flopped out of her ripped open stomach and without the need to run, Melanie was present when the foul stench of the old woman's piss and shit wafted her way.

It all seemed to happen so slowly like all the evil she'd done to Melanie's friends was put back on her tenfold. She was paying for it in slow motion.

By the time Melanie snapped out of her stupor and remembered the final part of her plan, the beast was nearly finished feasting. If this didn't work, she knew she was setting herself up for certain death, but she couldn't leave here knowing this thing was on the loose.

She couldn't walk away knowing another group of college kids or an innocent commuter like Mike could be torn apart by this monster.

It was her duty to try.

Her fingers were still sticky with the woman's blood, but they would be drying soon.

She took a few steps closer, to make sure she wasn't too far away.

"Hey!" she yelled at the beast.

It didn't respond.

Much like when she threw the tire iron at it while it was eating Tucker, the beast ignored her.

"Hey, look at me!" she tried again.

The beast growled and sniffed the air. It glanced toward her, and it was all the time she needed but it was also long enough to almost make her change her mind. The creepy, chubby, childlike face scared the hell out of her.

She lifted the camera with a grimace as she snapped the picture.

The beast flinched in the light, but it didn't attack. Instead, it went back to munching on its mother.

Melanie waited for the photo to pop out and when the image developed, she couldn't believe it. It was crystal clear. She had proof that the monster existed. She didn't know if this would work, but it was worth a try. Using her blood-smeared finger, she circled the beast's face with blood.

The beast stopped eating and went silent.

It sniffed and whined.

Melanie decided now was the time to walk away. If it came after her, she would rather have her back turned and be unaware.

She was halfway to the visitor center doors when she heard the beast's howl. Then it let out one of its strange childlike howls. It shrieked.

Then the sounds it let out were like nothing she'd ever heard before.

When she glanced back, she saw a gory mess she'd never get out of her mind. The creature was tearing into its chest and throat with its claws. It bit down on its forearm and chewed its hand off.

It was on a mission to destroy itself.

She watched it hit its knees and tear into its other arm, crying out with each bite but continuing to eat.

Melanie turned from the sight and hurried through the visitor center doors. First, she stopped by the old man's body. Clem was his name; she'd always remember that. She reached into his pocket, hoping the old woman hadn't taken his keys. Luckily, she must have forgotten that in her grieving. The keys were there. Melanie took them.

Next, she went into the visitor center. Mitch was still alive but badly injured. She went into his office, found his cell phone, and brought it to him.

"Here. The curse is over."

Sure, she felt bad for Mitch, but he had enough strength to call an ambulance. She wasn't willing to wait. The cops might arrive quickly. An ambulance might, too.

That crazy-ass congregation from the Church of Hezekiah Downs might show up too, and that wasn't something she was willing to risk. She knew if she drove herself to the nearest police station, she was taking matters into her own hands.

No, not the nearest police station. I don't even trust that. They might be congregation members.

"Wha . . . where are you going?" Mitch asked as she walked out of the visitor center.

"Home, Mitch," Melanie said. "I'm going home."

Subscribe to Crystal Lake Publishing's
Dark Tide series for updates, specials,
behind-the-scenes content, and a
special selection of bonus stories
- http://eepurl.com/hKVGkr

THE END?

Not if you want to dive into more of the Dark Tide series.

Check out our amazing website and online store
or download our latest catalog here.
https://geni.us/CLPCatalog

We always have great new projects and content on the website to
dive into, as well as a newsletter, behind the scenes options,
social media platforms, our own dark fiction shared-world series
and our very own webstore. Our webstore even has categories
specifically for KU books, non-fiction, anthologies, and of course
more novels and novellas.

ABOUT THE AUTHORS

Rowland Bercy Jr. burst onto the writing scene just three years ago, and has quickly established himself as a talented storyteller. His novella Unbortion was met with both acclaim and controversy, earning him top honors at the 2020 American Fiction Awards and a finalist spot in the 2019 International Book Awards. Readers who seek to push their own boundaries while delving into the darker aspects of life will find his work exciting and rewarding.

Rowland's writing experience has been a rollercoaster ride of excitement and uncertainty, taking him on an adventure unlike any other. Throughout his journey, he encountered numerous talented authors and many devoted fans who have motivated and supported him every step of the way.

He can be found on social media platforms like Facebook, Instagram, and Tik Tok, as well as on his website: www.rowlandbercyjr.com

Lucas Mangum is the author of nearly twenty books, spanning from splatterpunk and extreme horror to cosmic horror and dark fantasy. He lives in Central Texas with his family and their pet bearded dragon. Subscribe to his newsletter at LucasMangum.Substack.com or check out his YouTube channel LMHorror.

Carver Pike is a three-time Splatterpunk Award-nominated horror author. He hosts his own YouTube show called, *First Chapter Freakshow*, where he reads other horror authors' books and talks about the world of indie horror publishing.

Pike wields his virtual pen and slings ink onto the page from his home in West Virginia where the people are friendly, the scenery is gorgeous, and horror story inspiration is in every nook, cranny, and holler.

As a Christian, a man of faith who writes some pretty messed up stories, he wants to create some of the vilest creatures you'd ever imagine, so you and he can slay them together.

Readers . . .

Thank you for reading *Hunted Highways*. We hope you enjoyed this 12th book in our Dark Tide series.

If you have a moment, please review *Hunted Highways* at the store where you bought it.

Help other readers by telling them why you enjoyed this book. No need to write an in-depth discussion. Even a single sentence will be greatly appreciated. Reviews go a long way to helping a book sell, and is great for an author's career. It'll also help us to continue publishing quality books. You can also share a photo of yourself holding this book with the hashtag #IGotMyCLPBook!

Thank you again for taking the time to journey with Crystal Lake Publishing.

Visit our Linktree page for a list of our social media platforms. https://linktr.ee/CrystalLakePublishing

Follow us on Amazon:

Our Mission Statement:

Since its founding in August 2012, Crystal Lake Publishing has quickly become one of the world's leading publishers of Dark Fiction and Horror books. In 2023, Crystal Lake Publishing formed a part of Crystal Lake Entertainment, joining several other divisions, including Torrid Waters, Crystal Lake Comics, Crystal Lake Kids, and many more.

While we strive to present only the highest quality fiction and entertainment, we also endeavour to support authors along their writing journey. We offer our time and experience in non-fiction projects, as well as author mentoring and services, at competitive prices.

With several Bram Stoker Award wins and many other wins and nominations (including the HWA's Specialty Press Award), Crystal Lake Publishing puts integrity, honor, and respect at the forefront of our publishing operations.

We strive for each book and outreach program we spearhead to not only entertain and touch or comment on issues that affect our readers, but also to strengthen and support the Dark Fiction field and its authors.

Not only do we find and publish authors we believe are destined for greatness, but we strive to work with men and women who endeavour to be decent human beings who care more for others than themselves, while still being hard working, driven, and passionate artists and storytellers.

Crystal Lake Publishing is and will always be a beacon of what passion and dedication, combined with overwhelming teamwork and respect, can accomplish. We endeavour to know each and every one of our readers, while building personal relationships with our authors, reviewers, bloggers, podcasters, bookstores, and libraries.

We will be as trustworthy, forthright, and transparent as any business can be, while also keeping most of the headaches away from our authors, since it's our job to solve the problems so they can stay in a creative mind. Which of course also means paying our authors.

We do not just publish books, we present to you worlds within your world, doors within your mind, from talented authors who sacrifice so much for a moment of your time.

There are some amazing small presses out there, and through collaboration and open forums we will continue to support other presses in the goal of helping authors and showing the world what quality small presses are capable of accomplishing. No one wins when a small press goes down, so we will always be there to support hardworking, legitimate presses and their authors. We don't see Crystal Lake as the best press out there, but we will always strive to be the best, strive to be the most interactive and grateful, and even blessed press around. No matter what happens over time, we will also take our mission very seriously while appreciating where we are and enjoying the journey.

What do we offer our authors that they can't do for themselves through self-publishing?

We are big supporters of self-publishing (especially hybrid publishing), if done with care, patience, and planning. However, not every author has the time or inclination to do market research, advertise, and set up book launch strategies. Although a lot of authors are successful in doing it all, strong small presses will always be there for the authors who just want to do what they do best: write.

What we offer is experience, industry knowledge, contacts and trust built up over years. And due to our strong brand and trusting fanbase, every Crystal Lake Publishing book comes with weight of respect. In time our fans begin to trust our judgment and will try a new author purely based on our support of said author.

With each launch we strive to fine-tune our approach, learn from our mistakes, and increase our reach. We continue to assure our authors that we're here for them and that we'll carry the weight of the launch and dealing with third parties while they focus on their strengths—be it writing, interviews, blogs, signings, etc.

We also offer several mentoring packages to authors that include knowledge and skills they can use in both traditional and self-publishing endeavours.

We look forward to launching many new careers.

This is what we believe in. What we stand for. This will be our legacy.

Welcome to Crystal Lake Publishing— Tales from the Darkest Depths.

Printed in Great Britain
by Amazon

38521939R00116